"I need help!"

A split second later another voice came over the radio. "Striker, this is Mowry. We're near your original drop zone. Make it back there and we'll take care of you."

"I'm telling you," Bolan shouted. "You need some heavy guns for this thing."

"We took care of the freaking aliens, didn't we?" Mowry said. "And we'll take care of this thing."

Bolan had no choice. It was coming and it was coming fast.

He continued his zigzag retreat through the bodies on the tunnel floor, hopping over the blood-slick carcasses as fast as he could move. Just as he reached the tunnel borer, the first sounds of gunfire echoed down the long chamber.

By then he was flat on his stomach, scrambling toward safety. He clamped one hand on the large treads and then vaulted behind the tunneler, using it as a giant shield.

He caught a glimpse of the second tunnel borer just as it rounded the corner. It chewed and burned its way through walls of stone and then headed toward the Executioner.

As he waited for its inevitable approach, Bolan wondered if the light at the end of the tunnel would be the last thing he ever saw.

MACK BOLAN ®
The Executioner

DON PENDLETON'S
THE EXECUTIONER®
UFORCE

A GOLD EAGLE BOOK FROM
WORLDWIDE®

TORONTO • NEW YORK • LONDON
AMSTERDAM • PARIS • SYDNEY • HAMBURG
STOCKHOLM • ATHENS • TOKYO • MILAN
MADRID • WARSAW • BUDAPEST • AUCKLAND

First edition August 2001
ISBN 0-373-64273-3

Special thanks and acknowledgment to
Rich Rainey for his contribution to this work.

UFORCE

Printed in U.S.A.

There is genuine scientific paydirt in UFOs and alien abductions—but it is, I think, of a distinctly homegrown and terrestrial character.

—Carl Sagan, *The Demon-Haunted World*

...The old gods have sailed their celestial barks right up to the doorstep of the computer generation, only instead of dragon-headed ships their vessels are space ships...

—Michael Talbot, *The Holographic Universe*

The truth is out there, but it's wearing a mask.

—Mack Bolan

For S.K., who's been there.

San Luis Valley, Colorado

The black triangular craft sailed soundlessly through the upper atmosphere high above the rugged Colorado mountains. It was cloaked in otherworldly ambient camouflage that painted its outside surface in a constantly shifting palette of colors to blend with its surroundings.

Now it was the color of night.

The stealth craft dropped like a stone for several thousand feet, then stopped suddenly and soundlessly as it hovered high above the San Luis Valley, the enormous corridor that stretched down through Colorado and deep into New Mexico.

It was time for the weekly run. Time to be seen by the inhabitants of the towns and ranches and resorts in all parts of the valley.

Hundreds, sometimes thousands of awestruck callers would flood the phone circuits with news of their latest UFO sighting. The calls inevitably overwhelmed the lightly staffed radio stations, newspapers and the volunteers at CUFOW, the Colorado UFO Web that kept an ever growing database of the sightings.

Other calls would go to county sheriff departments. Depending on the intensity of the call or credibility of the witnesses, the sheriffs would occasionally pass the information up through channels until it reached "the mountain," NORAD's tomblike headquarters buried deep inside Cheyenne Mountain.

Few of the reports would ever match.

It always seemed like a dozen types of crafts were flying

the night skies over Colorado. The triangular craft could present countless different shapes or signatures to the watchers below. Or it could assume no shape at all.

With a sudden rush of wind the black triangle soared across the valley.

It was in whisper mode. Virtually silent, observing but unobserved.

A dark metallic predator that owned the night.

Gideon, New Mexico

KENNETH TAYLOR, hatchet man for the government accounting office, was about to join the ranks of a very exclusive fraternity. He was the only man in the room unaware that soon he would embark on a life-changing course.

The two other men hid their intentions behind respectful faces and pleasant but meaningless conversation. The subterfuge came naturally to them after years of dealing with senators and CEOs, black budgets and black operations.

"We understand your position," Colonel Goddard said, rising from his desk to signal the meeting was over. "No hard feelings."

He leaned across his desk to shake the younger man's hand. Taylor's grip barely registered, the result of pushing too many calculator buttons. Goddard's steely grip was the product of almost six decades of conquest. It was the hand of a man who reached out and grabbed for the brass ring every time.

"You're taking this quite well, Colonel," Taylor said, flexing his fingers when the colonel released his hand.

"It was inevitable," Goddard said. "We've expected cutbacks for some time now and are prepared to do what we must."

"Glad you see it that way," the government investigator said, still surprised at how calmly the head of Project UFORCE received the bad news. He'd driven out to Goddard's isolated administrative headquarters to seal the fate of an operation that had gone unchecked for far too long.

From this three-story building that looked like a control tower in the desert, Goddard maintained a covert apparatus with divisions all across the southwestern United States. Perhaps he'd branched out even farther, Taylor thought. So many assets were missing it was hard to tell what he'd done with them.

Though Taylor used diplomatic terms like "cost overruns" and "misplaced matériel" instead of "rampant theft," both sides knew why the project was getting the ax. And they both knew it wouldn't just be downsized. It was finished.

UFORCE personnel would be reassigned, assets relocated or liquidated, and soon Goddard himself would have to abandon the sinking ship.

"Captain Stevenson will see you out," Goddard said, nodding to the physically imposing aide who led the GAO inspector on his earlier tour of the site and answered all questions with remarkable candor.

"This way, Ken," Stevenson said, ushering him through the door.

On the way to the elevator Taylor felt as if he were in the other man's shadow. Stevenson was a full head taller than Taylor and even in his perfectly fitted suit looked as if he'd been bred for battle. His thick brown mustache was precisely groomed, and he had a perfect set of teeth that flashed in an easy smile.

Taylor disliked him from the moment they met. It wasn't just jealousy of his looks. Stevenson's mental sharpness was just as intimidating as his strength.

Without having to look up anything even once, Stevenson had answered all of Taylor's questions about the UFORCE operation. Mission statements. Manpower. Inventory. Project man-hours. Ethernet capacity. He provided a blizzard of statistics without hesitation.

And though Stevenson never wrote down anything, he demonstrated a total recall of every word that Taylor had spoken, whether it was a code number or the name of an obscure GAO official back in Washington.

A typical intelligence man, Taylor thought. Stevenson soaked up everything he could about his business and yours. A walking computer who knew more about you than you could ever guess about him.

While they waited for the elevator to come to the third floor, Stevenson was totally relaxed, ready to deal with anything that came his way. It was Taylor who felt ill at ease. He'd come here to pronounce a death sentence on the apparatus they'd built up for decades. Yet neither Stevenson nor Goddard seemed too upset. Perhaps it was their guilt, he thought. Maybe they really had been expecting this for a long time.

Taylor looked at the indicator lights and willed the elevator to hurry. Finally the car arrived with a soft clunking sound and the doors hissed open. He stepped inside ahead of Stevenson.

Suddenly he felt as if he had to get out of there. It was claustrophobic in the small car. The feeling grew worse when the door shut and Stevenson's large presence filled all the space. He wondered what his chances would be if he ever had to try to get past someone like Stevenson. The answer came immediately. Zero.

The cabin lurched downward with a swift and nauseating plunge. He felt light-headed suddenly. Clammy forehead. Tightness in his chest. What had he been thinking? Coming out here alone to a desert outpost, an unwanted messenger in an enemy camp. He wondered if they had slipped him something.

"Is everything okay?" Stevenson said, turning to face him.

"Yes. Of course. Why?"

"You just looked uncomfortable for a moment. Could be the elevation's getting to you. It gives some people headaches. Shortness of breath."

The door opened up on the first floor. "No," he said, breathing easier. "I'm fine."

"Good," Stevenson said, giving him another hearty smile.

He walked with him past a uniformed security guard, then stopped at the corridor that led down to the parking garage.

"Here's where we part company," Stevenson said. "If you have any further questions, don't hesitate to ask. I'll be here as long as you need me."

"I'll do that," Taylor said, shaking his hand, smiling and promising himself he'd have no more contact with either man. As soon as his recommendation reached the right ears, a team of federal agents and accountants would come out here to shut them down.

He stepped into the halogen-lit garage, got into his government-issue sedan and drove through the paved lot to the earthen road that led away from the bureaucratic nightmare that was UFORCE. He flicked on his high beams, increasing the field of vision on the flat desert road.

About a mile away from the three-story complex, he started to feel a bit better. His breathing was a lot easier now that the hard part of the job was over with. He'd stayed longer than he'd expected, working into the night.

But now he could relax a bit. He popped a classic jazz tape into the dashboard player, adjusted the volume, then pressed down on the pedal. He had a lot of ground to cover.

Midway into Dexter Gordon's first solo, he picked up the cellular phone.

Nothing. It was dead.

That couldn't be, he thought. It worked fine on the way out here. The battery was charged and the power cord was still hooked into the cigarette lighter. He thumbed the on button several times, but the LED screen stayed dark.

Too bad. He wanted to make a preliminary report while everything was fresh in his memory.

And he had to admit, he was feeling a bit spooked.

COLONEL GODDARD STOOD by the window of his third-floor office and watched the fading red taillights vanish into the New Mexico night.

His neck was ramrod straight and his hands were clasped

behind his back, almost as if he were about to address the troops. In a way he was. From this moment on, UFORCE was on a war footing.

It was unavoidable. It was tragic. But it was necessary. UFORCE had a charter to defend the country against its enemies. Sometimes those enemies were abroad. Sometimes they were right in your own backyard.

Goddard turned away from the window and pressed a one-touch number on his desktop scramble unit. The other party picked up immediately, as if he'd been waiting just for this call.

"Yes?" the voice said.

"Unleash the falcons," Goddard said.

San Luis Valley, Colorado

THE BLACK TRIANGLE GLIDED slowly across the valley at one hundred feet above the ground. It decelerated to a five-mile-per-hour crawl over Rainbow Ridge, the red-stone-and-crystal-specked cliffs outside the small town of Crystal Springs.

Several cars and pickup trucks were parked on the lip of the ridge, looking out over the valley as if it were a cosmic drive-in. Nearly every night a small crowd came out to the ridge in hopes of another UFO sighting. The ridge had a history of being a UFO hot spot. Sometimes strange lights were seen three times a week. Other times it was once a month. No one could tell when the ships would come.

KAREN SOMMERFIELD SHOOK her head as she studied the look of rapture on Deputy M. L. Waters's face. He sat behind the steering wheel of his Ford Explorer and stared out at the empty sky as if she weren't even there.

"You've got to be kidding," she said. "You really took me out here to look for lights in the sky?"

"Sure. What'd you expect?"

"More than this," she said. She'd expected their relationship to move up a notch when he asked her to come out to the ridge. It was a perfect night for romance and she had tomorrow off. The *Crystal Springs Weekly* had printed the latest edition, and everyone could take a breath for a day or two.

They'd gone out a few times since she moved there for the reporting job, fresh out of college and determined to make a name for herself. Covering town meetings and writing cow copy. And maybe even the strange lights in the sky.

"Oh, my God," she said.

"What?"

"There it is."

He followed her pointing finger. One moment there was nothing but dark skies. Suddenly a black metal manta ray blinked into existence.

It filled the horizon, huge and silent, sailing in front of the cliff so close and slow that it seemed as if she could reach out and touch it. It drifted back and forth almost as if it wanted to be seen by the long row of cars and pickups lined up on the ridge.

Beneath the triangular wings a phalanx of bright white lights flicked on and illuminated the dark underside of the ship.

Just like all the reports said, Karen thought.

The lights changed color in an almost hypnotic sequence, pulsing bright green and red and then back to white again.

With a sudden burst of speed it darted around like a planchette on a Ouija board, moving up and down and diagonally in sharp angles.

A loud thunderclap shook the ridge and lightning shot across the sky. The ship was gone. All that was left behind was a searing afterimage that temporarily blinded anyone who looked too long.

As if waking from a dream, Karen reached into her purse and took out a memo pad and pencil. She had come out to Colorado hoping to find something to write about. And now it had found her.

Gideon, New Mexico

HEADLIGHTS APPEARED in his rearview mirror a half hour after Taylor left Goddard. He flicked the mirror to its night-driving position to dampen the glare, then stepped on the gas pedal to put some distance between them.

But the lights bore down on him quickly. Within half a minute they filled the inside of the car with a harsh yellow brightness that made him feel like a target.

The lights blinked out suddenly. And in his mirror he saw the dark shadowed windshield of the car behind him. Tailgating him.

When the driver blew his horn just inches from his bumper, the sound made him jump.

Christ, he thought. Just what he needed. A psychotic desert rat on a dark desolate road stretching on to infinity. And his car phone was dead. He could try to outrace them, but he didn't know the road well enough for that.

The demented driver let loose with another long blast of the horn, then pulled into the passing lane.

It was a black Cadillac. An old model from the sixties. Large fins, lots of chrome. There were at least three men inside the vehicle.

It rode even with him, then surged slightly ahead so the man in the back seat was even with Taylor. The gaunt-faced man glared at Taylor with a cadaverous gaze. His corpse-like eyes never moved, as if they were locked on to his with a ghostly radar.

Taylor shuddered and looked away. The Caddy shot forward, then bounced down the dirt road, going at least eighty miles per hour.

He exhaled loudly and loosened his white-knuckled grip on the steering wheel. His hands had been anchored there ever since the chase car appeared. Chase car. The thought came out of the blue. Did Goddard send someone after him? No, he thought. The man wouldn't try anything so foolish. Would he?

Within ten minutes the episode with the Caddy faded from his mind. He was cruising along at a good speed and far behind him he saw the high headlights of a freight truck. Good, he was no longer alone on the road.

In another half hour he'd be on the interstate, heading back to civilization.

He felt fine—until a dark shape blacked out the stars in front of him. To the left and right he saw the star-filled sky. But dead ahead a massive triangular shape hovered above the road like a black ceiling lowering down on his world. A UFO.

He started to slow down, but then the night fell upon him.

A jolt of electricity surged through the car. Clicking and buzzing sounds wrapped it in an arcing blue aura.

The engine died. The headlights failed. And the car rolled to a stop.

Taylor peered through the windshield just as a bright beam shot from the black triangle. There was a fluttering, humming sound in his eardrums, like triggers going off. His eyes were bathed by a pulsing light that was like nothing he'd ever seen before, like nothing on earth.

Taylor stopped thinking. He stopped being. He fell into the side of his seat like an empty container. Fell into darkness.

Something woke him a short time later. He couldn't tell if seconds or minutes passed before he heard the tapping at the window. He groaned and forced himself to sit up. He saw long gray fingers tapping at the glass. Then a face with black almond-shaped eyes peered in. They looked out from a round gray skull.

Taylor's shriek filled the car with a maddening echo, a scream that lasted until something on the other side of the car broke through the window and reached inside.

Another gray being. As he looked toward the newcomer, he felt a stinging sensation at the back of his neck. Then his blood froze and he blacked out—forever.

THE FREIGHT TRUCK STOPPED in the middle of the road just as the black Cadillac drove back and parked nose to nose with Taylor's sedan.

One of the occupants from the Cadillac got out, walked to

the back of the truck, levered open the doors and slid a white metal ramp down to the ground.

A second occupant got behind the wheel of Taylor's car, started the engine on the first try, and drove it up the ramp into the truck.

One minute later the truck pulled back onto the road, followed by the Caddy.

Kenneth Taylor had vanished from the face of the earth.

2

Near the San Isabel National Forest, Colorado

A dry mountain breeze drifted across the high desert canyon that sheltered the man known as the Executioner.

His sand-colored khakis blended in with the rock-strewed gully that bordered the home of Dr. Lincoln Sturges.

Mack Bolan had been observing it for several hours now. It was a modern two-story structure with solar panels, sky-lights—and an underground shelter.

After all, the reclusive consultant for the U.S. Army Corps of Engineers was the brains behind the construction of several secret underground bases across the United States. For the past three decades Sturges was involved in scouting, planning and designing hardsites and tunnel complexes for the Army, Air Force and the Federal Emergency Management Agency.

That made him an extremely important man to the covert community.

It also made him a target for UFORCE, the agency that had often tapped his expertise—before it went rogue.

Although Sturges had always maintained secrecy about the location of his Colorado home near the San Isabel National Forest, there was no way it could stay hidden from professional spooks for too long. It was only a matter of time before the rogue agency sent someone to pay a visit to Sturges.

The Executioner would be there to meet any intruders.

Slowly he moved down the gully, crouching beneath the rock overhang to shield himself from the sun and from any possible high-altitude-surveillance net UFORCE had dropped on the site.

Bolan still wasn't sure exactly what the technical capacity of Project UFORCE was. There hadn't been much time during the briefing with Hal Brognola to go over every single detail. The director of Sensitive Operations Group had set up a temporary command post at Kirtland Air Force Base down in Albuquerque where he was busy launching other strike teams all across the four-corner area of the Southwest.

The uncanny border shared by the corners of Utah, Arizona, Colorado and New Mexico happened to be the center of some of the most restricted and advanced military activity in the United States.

It was also the center of Project UFORCE, whose very existence and operations were a well-guarded secret.

The apparent defection of the underground agency had sent shock waves through Washington. The White House had enlisted trusted covert chieftains like Hal Brognola to assess the damage and contain the threat as discreetly as possible. Instead of an all-out attack, they had to operate on a clandestine basis.

That was the problem with UFORCE. No one really knew how far its tentacles reached. It had succeeded far too well in creating a covert strike force that couldn't be traced to the U.S. government.

Somewhere along the way it mutated, or evolved, depending on where you stood. Colonel Goddard had planted assets and allies through the military and intelligence establishment. At this point there was no way of knowing how many highly placed officers and agents were loyal to the colonel. Until he had a better scorecard, Brognola was relying on those he could trust with his life.

Men like the Executioner.

Bolan scanned the horizon through a compact monocular that could fit in the palm of his hands when it was folded up. In its extended position it gave him a clear field of vision well past one thousand yards. He swept the eyepiece across the foothills, then traced the shoulder of the red rock plateau.

Nothing moved.

Yet.

He was sure they would come. Probably by nightfall.

During the past few days several people connected to the investigation of UFORCE had disappeared, committed suicide, or suffered unusual accidents. No doubt Dr. Sturges was overdue for a similar accident.

A movement in his peripheral vision brought Bolan's scope back to the house. On the second floor a silhouette was moving behind the sliding glass door that led to a wraparound deck.

It was the silhouette of a tall and gangly man about the same height as Sturges.

But it wasn't the doctor. Sturges was under armed guard in a safehouse a hundred miles away.

It was Sergeant Vince Mowry, a Special Forces operative who found himself attached to many of Brognola's operations during these past few years. His job was to make sure the desert home still looked inhabited.

Mowry had the lanky frame of a marathon runner, and from a distance that gave him a remarkable resemblance to Sturges. No one would notice the difference until he got up close. But by then it wouldn't matter.

Mowry was the decoy.

Bolan was the early-warning system.

Rather than field a heavy force that would deter an attack, they wanted to bring UFORCE out into the open.

The Executioner scanned the area one more time, then snapped the lightweight monocular shut and let it hang from his neck like a dog tag.

He waited for night to fall.

BOLAN FELT a brief sense of disbelief come over him when he saw the craft hovering above the plateau.

Even his firsthand experience with stealth craft hadn't prepared him for this. He knew about the cloaking and sound-suppressing technology, but he'd seen nothing like this before.

It was totally silent, a shifting chimera that seemed to change color and shape the longer he looked at it. Sometimes it seemed to be a totally black triangular object, while at other times the underside of the craft appeared to be painted with stars, a shimmering digital screensaver that cloaked it with cosmic camouflage.

Bolan fished the CommPak from his vest, hooked up the tiny earpiece, then looked down at the digital read-out screen. The satellite-fed 500 MB memory device showed an overhead view of the surrounding land features.

But it showed nothing in the sky.

The Executioner looked skyward again and saw that the unidentified object was still there. It was drifting in closer now, a predator swooping in on prey.

Bolan tapped a button that refreshed the screen with several different touch-screen icons. He thumbed the icon that shared a link with both Mowry and the command-and-control group set up by Brognola in Kirtland AFB.

"This is Striker One," Bolan said into the speaker built into the CommPak's front grip. "There is an unknown craft moving across the range. Is it one of ours?" His words were converted to a scrambled signal that was immediately decoded by similar units held by the other members of the team.

The response came almost immediately in Bolan's miniature earpiece. "This is Control, Striker. Negative to your sighting. We have no craft in the area at this time. I repeat, we have no craft in the area. The bogey is not showing up on our screens."

"Mine, neither," Bolan said. "But something damn well is flying up there." He kept his gaze on the black craft as it closed the gap. "The naked eye is receiving it just fine. Get ready, doc, it's coming in."

"Roger," Mowry replied. "I'll be waiting."

"This is Control, we are—"

The earpiece went dead.

Bolan tried contacting the team again, but there was no response. All communications had suddenly shut down as if a blanket of silence had shrouded the area.

He looked up and caught one more glimpse of the floating

craft as it neared Sturges's house. It was moving slowly, the nose of the craft angling toward the heavens like a dull black diamond scraping the sky.

A hatch opened beneath the craft. Several tendril-like ropes dropped to the rooftop and dark shapes rapidly slid down. The figures slowly spread out along the rooftop and the triangle blinked out of existence.

Mowry was under attack.

Bolan jogged downhill, stepping carefully over the smooth round boulders that lined the bottom of the gully.

He was carrying a small arsenal, including the familiar and dependable Beretta 93-R in the underarm holster rig. He'd brought it with him in case he needed to go in silently. But he also had another weapon slung over his shoulder that he instinctively went for as he neared the end of the gully.

Silence wasn't going to be a major factor now that an invading force was knocking on the doctor's skylight.

Bolan hooked his thumb into the shoulder strap and shrugged the P-90 Fabrique Nationale pistol off his shoulder. The short-muzzled Special Forces weapon could serve as a machine pistol, submachine gun or assault rifle with the retracted stock.

This night the Executioner was more interested in its stopping power than its flexibility. With the 50-round horizontal magazine, the 5.7 mm rounds could do a lot of stopping.

He took one step out into the open before the voice warned him.

It was his inner voice, the subconscious battle sense that kept him alive all these years. Any craft that could drop invaders so quietly onto a rooftop could have just as easily dropped off another team to sweep through the foothills.

Bolan dived forward into the darkness just as a burst of automatic fire strafed the top of the gully where he'd been a moment ago.

He landed hard on the ground, clutching the FN P-90 as he skidded across the rocky terrain. Short bursts of sound-suppressed fire chopped the air overhead as he rolled toward a jagged spine of rock that offered the only possible cover.

Bolan glimpsed the fading barrel-flashes from the hills behind him and opened up with several short bursts of return fire. The 5.7 mm rounds drilled into the soft hillside and at least one of the invaders.

His fatal cry of surprise stopped suddenly as his lungs filled with blood and he went down.

They'd come here expecting easy prey. A scientist and maybe some rent-a-cops. Instead they found themselves face-to-face with a warrior.

Bolan triggered a sustained burst that sprayed the hillside from left to right, burning off the rest of the clip to keep the strike team down and buy himself a little more time.

At least one of them was out of action, he thought. He might have hit another one. But how many more were out there?

He'd seen four, possibly five muzzle-flashes spearing the darkness. Maybe they'd all fired. Or maybe a second part of the team had held its fire and was moving on him now.

He heard scuttling movement and a number of voices shouting back and forth as the team regrouped and planned his demise. It was a very simple plan. They were coming after him in a head-on attack.

Bolan could hear their feet scrambling over the rough ground, heading toward the gully he'd just come from. They'd simply follow it to the end and flush him out. Bolan took stock of his position. He was on the bottom of a rocky slope facing an unknown number of gunners.

The expected thing would be to fall back into the clearing between here and Sturges's house. But there was almost no cover to be found. Just some brush and a few depressions in the high grass. Even if he made it to the field, there was little chance he'd make it to the house. They'd just turn it into a fox hunt and beat the bushes until one of them got him.

He slapped a fresh magazine into the FN P-90, took a deep breath just long enough to gather his wits and then ran for the gully.

Muffled bursts broke through the temporary quiet that had fallen over the killing field. Bullets hummed through the air above him and ricocheted off the rock he'd sought shelter behind.

Bolan lurched forward, keeping low to the ground and moving left and right as his feet pounded the dirt and he literally raced for his life.

He kept running when he made it to the mouth of the gully. One thing in his favor was his familiarity with the narrow trench that zigzagged its way up through the foothills. He knew the turns and depressions and the long straight stretches.

Bolan scrambled up the gully toward the strategic landmark he'd noticed before, an extremely narrow passage where the gully made an almost ninety-degree turn. He pressed his back into the hard clay, rested the short barrel of the 50-round pistol against the dirt wall behind him, then reached into the side pocket of his combat vest.

"He's over there," a man's voice said. "I heard him stop."

"Got it," a second man replied.

"Let's take him."

The hard-edged voices belonged to men who'd obviously done this kind of work before, men who now had a comrade to avenge.

Bolan heard their approach down the gully. This group was counting on quickness, not quiet.

And he also heard the furtive movements of at least one other man walking farther up the crest of the gully. A backup man, tasked with taking Bolan out when the others engaged him in gunfire.

The footsteps of several men sounded throughout the gully, stopping at the end of the corridor just around the bend.

Clumps of dirt exploded from the side of the gully directly opposite from Bolan's face. Another sustained burst thumped into the rocky wall and sprayed the Executioner with shards of clay. Just like dirt falling into a grave.

Slowly the attackers made their way down the corridor, reconning by fire at every twist and turn.

They stopped for a moment, preparing for the final charge.

Bolan listened to them start to climb carefully over the same ground he'd covered before. He could pinpoint where they were just by gauging the closeness of their footsteps.

Now.

He cocked his arm and released the thermite grenade with a gentle underhanded motion that tossed it around the bend.

It fell like a rock at their feet.

They stopped dead in their tracks, wasting a vital few moments registering the threat before they turned and ran. But it was too late. The tremendous explosion lifted them off the ground like human rockets, airborne and in flames. Their screams raced with the concussive roar that echoed through the gully and bounced across the hills.

The blast filled the corridor with a ribbon of fire that instantly took out every man as if Bolan had cleared the trench with a flame thrower.

Just to make certain, Bolan edged the barrel of the FN P-90 around the sharp corner and strafed the pathway. Sensing movement from above, he nosed the barrel skyward and sheared the top off another man's skull just as he was aiming his weapon at Bolan.

The UFORCE assassin dropped down into the gully with his last thoughts pouring out of him in a damp flood of red.

Bolan quietly back-stepped to the mouth of the gully. He stopped at a vantage point that gave him a good look up the rest of the slope.

Nothing was moving. He crept over the lip of the gully and headed uphill to make sure it stayed that way.

He thought about helping Mowry, but it would be foolish to head for the house until he knew the field was clear. Bolan wouldn't be much help to the other man if he caught a bullet in the back.

Besides, Mowry was a decoy, not a sitting duck.

SERGEANT MOWRY HAD FELT the stillness descending above the house. First there was a rushing-wind motion as if a high-pressure system were pressing down upon the room. Then there was quiet.

The quiet before the storm.

He heard them dropping to the rooftop. Rappelling down. First he heard the ropes hitting the roof, then the soft footfalls of the men sliding down.

They spread out on the roof, ready to break in or scale down the side of the house.

The ship had come in, and Mowry had to deal with the crew.

He stepped back into one of the dark bedrooms and picked up the rapid-fire room sweeper he'd loaded with high-explosive cartridges, fléchette rounds and flash shells. Even with the loaded drum magazine, the selective-fire shotgun could theoretically be fired with one hand, not that he favored shooting that way.

If he had to use the weapon, he wasn't going to pick anyone off with a pistol shot. He was going for maximum firepower.

The first round was a Starflash cartridge, designed to stun unwanted guests long enough to determine whether they were terminal risks. The next rounds were designed to finish them off if necessary.

He carried the shotgun back into the hallway and leaned against the wall. Then he aimed the remote-control unit he'd been carrying around with him all day long. It controlled the television, the track light, the thermostat, the main house computer and the receding skylight built into the ceiling. A touch of the button would turn the ceiling into an observatory.

Perhaps because of all of the time he spent underground, Sturges was a stargazer. Good, Mowry thought. That would give him a clear view of the intruders.

Mowry waited patiently for the assault team. The intruders went about their business as if they had all the time in the world and had no worries about the man below. As far as they were concerned, they had the doctor all boxed up in his high desert mousetrap, ready to cart him off or put him under.

Mowry clicked a button on the remote and plunged the house into darkness. Then he pressed a second button.

With a gentle whir the ceiling panels opened up. Starlight spilled into the room as the panels retracted into the side walls and revealed the glass ceiling.

Beams of light shot down through the clear pane and danced across the floor, giving Mowry a good look at his intruders.

The sight rooted him at the spot.

Several black-clad shapes had jumped back as soon as the panels opened. They stood there looking down through the glass as if it were a fishbowl, scanning the room with the flashlight beams mounted on their automatic weapons. None of them had seen Mowry yet.

But it wasn't the men in black who caught his attention. In the diffused light from the beams, Mowry saw a gray figure with black almond-shaped eyes. It stood rigid among the others and slowly moved its head to scan the room.

To lock eyes with Mowry.

Alien eyes.

The figure looked surprised. It stepped back, said something to the other shapes and then it was gone. A moment later he saw the black triangle rise into the sky.

He only caught a glimpse of it before a pair of heavy boots crashed through the glass, caving in the ceiling.

Mowry stayed back as giant spears of glass rained onto the floor, making a loud sound as they splintered into thousands of pieces.

The intruder landed in the middle of the floor, slipped on the glass for a moment and then regained his balance. But then he lost it forever.

Mowry drew his 9 mm Colt and triggered two shots. The first round caught the gunner in the head, and the second chewed a hole in his chest while he was dropped backward. The submachine in the man's hand dropped unfired onto the glass.

Three other men fired down into the room before they jumped through the shattered opening.

By now they knew they weren't facing Sturges.

Mowry flipped on antiflash goggles and opened up with the shotgun.

Incandescent daylight spurted into the room with brilliant flashes catching the intruders unaware. The disorienting light burst purchased him a few moments of precious time.

The well-trained soldiers tried to recover from the shock and were bringing their weapons up toward the hall, ready to fire blindly at the source of the flash.

The shotgun fired first.

Flesh-shredding rounds blasted into the center of the room, ripping all three men off their feet and casting their flesh and blood and wounded souls onto the walls.

Mowry spun the barrel toward the hallway ceiling over his head and fired another round.

Plaster and wood erupted as the round exploded through the roof.

He walked down the hall, methodically firing single shots through the ceiling until he reached the staircase. Then he rapid-fired the rest of the drum and sent a barrage up through the roof.

Mowry ran down the stairs, listening to the shouts behind him as more intruders dropped through the trashed ceiling.

Following the rehearsed steps he'd taken several times during the afternoon, Mowry headed through the basement door. Just before he slammed the reinforced blast door, he clicked the remote once more and rolled down into the bunker.

It detonated a series of shaped charges that Mowry had carefully planted through the house. Struts and cross beams crashed down like dominoes as the explosions took out the walls and windows and every last intruder who took part in the attack on Sturges.

The target had become a tomb.

3

Gideon, New Mexico

The dull green C-130 Hercules troop transport flew across New Mexico airspace shortly before dawn, packed with bomb-disposal equipment, demolition experts and a small special-operations security force.

Their destination was the abandoned headquarters of Colonel Goddard.

Shortly after the disappearance of the GAO investigator who visited the site, Goddard's entire staff had also disappeared. They left behind an empty shell.

The fleet of company vehicles was missing. Most of the computers had been destroyed except for a few hard drives that were salvaged. Banks of filing cabinets on the second floor were booby trapped to go off as soon as they were opened. That was discovered the hard way by the first Army CID agents on the scene. One of them was currently in the hospital with severe burns over most of his body.

The remaining members of the CID team had sealed off the building and called for help. Now they were waiting for the airdrop.

It was supposed to be a discreet operation. So far no one in the media had stumbled onto the strange incident that occurred at the anonymous-looking complex, and Hal Brognola wanted to keep it that way.

The drop sequence called for the troopers to make their jump on the first pass over the drop zone.

On the next pass the C-130 would fly low to the ground and release the cargo packages the crew had rigged for low-level parachute extraction. The parachutes would pull the cargo crates outside the rear door and drop them to the ground.

Then the CID recovery team would help the troops hustle the equipment out of the zone, and the transport plane would head home.

At least that was the plan.

In reality *everything* dropped from the sky at once.

The leader of the CID recovery team was waiting at the edge of the drop zone when he saw a bright flash in the sky.

A ball of flame seared the side of the transport plane just as it crested a ridge two miles east of the zone.

The plane cracked open and plummeted to the earth.

It landed with a tremendous crash and was obliterated in a billowing funnel of smoke and flame that incinerated every last soul aboard the doomed craft.

The explosion was heard for miles around.

Gideon was no longer a secret.

Albuquerque, New Mexico

THE COMMANDER of the COG joint task force was waiting for Bolan in a windowless and soundproofed office near the western perimeter of Kirtland Air Force Base. It was the same room where Brognola had previously set up shop and briefed both men and where the big Fed was supposed to debrief him now.

But there was no sign of him. The maps and dossiers that covered his desk were gone. So were his laptop computer and his portable communications net, proof that Brognola was no longer in residence.

"What's going on?" Bolan asked, surprised at the sight of Donovan Macauley sitting behind the desk. The soft-spoken but hard-eyed commander didn't look too happy to be there.

"Sit down, Striker," the commander said, gesturing at the chair that faced his desk.

Bolan dropped into the chair and took a sip of the over-cooked vending-machine coffee he brought with him. It was the first cup of the day and it tasted just bad enough to jolt his system and wake him up. He was still feeling the aftereffects of his long vigil out at Sturges's place and the encounter with the UFORCE team.

"The situation's changed since the last time we all met here," Macauley said. "We've got a major fuckup on our hands."

"So what's different?" Bolan asked.

"For one thing Brognola's not on the base anymore."

The news didn't sit well with Bolan, and he didn't bother to hide it. "And your Continuity of Government group's taking over for him?" Bolan suggested. "Is this supposed to be a hand-off?" The Executioner had come into this operation at the request of Hal Brognola. He wasn't happy about the possibility of being under someone else's control.

"You can relax, Striker. COG is still supporting Hal. We're pooling resources and sharing intelligence just like before. We're equals in this."

"Right," Bolan said, nodding at the commander like they were sharing an inside joke. From what he knew of COG operations, they seldom played a backup role. They led everyone to think so, but more often than not they were the ones in the driver's seat.

The COG task force was a little known covert group with a nationwide scope. Its charter was to keep the country running in times of a national emergency. It drew from all of the military services and from their intelligence brethren. Back in Washington the COG planning and logistics bureaucrats devised worst-case scenarios that could befall the government and then did their best to prevent them from happening.

They were the brains. Macauley was the brawn.

"What are you thinking, Striker?"

"I'm thinking I'd like to know where the hell Brognola is."

"He's gone underground," Macauley said. "He believes one of his operations may have been compromised and until he finds out where and how, he's going to be moving around a lot.''

"You know his location?" Bolan asked.

"I do."

"How?"

"I set it up for him."

"I'm not surprised," Bolan said sarcastically. "So what happens now? We communicate through carrier pigeon?"

Macauley shook his head. "You're still in the loop, Striker. Hal's locations will be provided to key individuals on a strict need-to-know basis. That includes you, me, some graybeards in our agency and a few higher-ups in the chain of command."

"Understood," Bolan said. "So where is he?"

Macauley reached into his pocket and took out a small black disk. "One of my people is bringing a car out front for you. As soon as you drive out through the gates, pop this disk into the dashboard computer. The display screen will map out the best way to Brognola's current location."

Bolan took the disk between his thumb and forefinger and waved it like a flag. "What about this?" he asked before dropping it into his shirt pocket. "Want me to toss it in a burn bag when I get there?"

"No need," the commander said. "It's good for one time only. Then it rewrites itself into a map that doesn't exist. The time code starts ticking as soon as you enable it, so don't get lost on the way."

"I won't," Bolan said, pocketing the disk. "I don't want to end up in the Twilight Zone."

Commander Macauley shook his head. "That's the problem," he said. "I'm afraid we're already there."

Macauley told him about the incident at the Gideon installation. Choppers from the same Special Operations Aviation Regiment—or SOAR—that brought Bolan and Mowry in from Sturges's place were now on their way to Gideon.

"We got one SOAR detachment flying in recovered bodies of the UFORCE attackers that you and Mowry tangled with. And we've got another detachment bringing back our own casualties from Gideon—what they can scrape off the ground, that is. We lost some damn good people out there. And this is only the beginning. I've got a feeling we're going to lose a lot more.''

Bolan listened to Macauley's account of the tragedy at Gideon. There was no smoking gun yet, but the feeling was that Goddard's people had somehow managed to plant an explosive device in with the bomb-disposal equipment. Or one of Goddard's troops fired a rocket at the C-130 as it flew low over the ridge. A forensic team was going over the ashes right now and a second, much more cautious crew was going through the office structure.

Whether they found proof or not, there was little doubt in either man's mind that the downing of the transport plane had been deliberate. The timing was too coincidental to consider it an accident.

It was the latest in a long line of accidents related to the UFORCE defection.

"Almost seems like Goddard knows exactly how your group would respond," Bolan said.

"That he does," Macauley agreed. "And with good reason. We worked side by side preparing ways the government could deal with catastrophic situations. No one ever thought that Goddard would turn out to be the worst catastrophe the government could ever face. And that's exactly what he is. He knows just about every play in the rule book.''

Macauley gave the Executioner a brief history of his previous dealings with Goddard in the early days. When they'd worked together, Project UFORCE was a mirror image of COG, but then it went deep black, and now no one was quite sure what it was.

"You didn't mention at the briefing that you knew him before.''

Macauley shrugged. "Didn't see the need at the time. You and Mowry were just one of several field teams who were shielding possible targets. We had to move fast to get you out in the field. A lot of teams got the green light. Some are still out there.''

''Are the other teams made up the same as ours?''

''Pretty much,'' Macauley said. ''Whenever possible we tried to match up one of Hal's top people with one of mine. Helps to keep both sides apprised of the situation.''

It also helped each of the chiefs keep an eye on the other, Bolan thought.

Macauley looked down at the desktop and smoothed his hands over the shiny surface. He had a faraway look in his eyes as if he were seeing the bodies of the men who crashed in the field. ''Back to the Gideon situation,'' he said. ''The crash of the C-130's going to be written up as a training accident. Exact same story's going out to the press and to the families. No one will like it and some of them will see through the cover story, but there's nothing they can do about it.''

''The families will know the real story,'' Bolan said. ''And they'll deal with it as best they can. It's the press that can cause problems.''

''Fuck the press,'' Macauley stated.

''Right.''

''I'm serious, Striker.''

''I don't follow you.''

''When I said fuck the press, I was merely passing on your orders.''

''Say again?''

''That's your cover,'' Macauley said. ''You're about to become a member in good standing of the press. We want you to find out which ones are working with Goddard and which ones will work with us.''

''What can a member of the press do?''

''A member of the UFO press,'' Macauley replied.

Bolan was about to protest when the commander smiled and said, ''Hal will fill you in more when you get there. After all, it was his idea.''

Macauley opened the desk drawer and took out some laminated IDs. "Here's your credentials." He tossed the packet across the desk.

Bolan looked at the press card that identified him as Gordon J. Miller, a reporter for a newspaper syndicate that was based in Washington, D.C.

"We know you normally use other aliases, but in this case we needed someone who had a credible past in the journalism field. It's a walk-in identity." He smiled enigmatically but didn't elaborate. "The Gordon Miller byline has appeared in countless newspapers, usually reporting on national events. But now and then the columns have shown an interest in esoteric subjects. Exactly the right background for a real journalist investigating arcane subjects like UFORCE and stealth craft."

"This has nothing to do with UFOs."

The COG commander smiled. "Nothing and everything. But again that's something to take up with Hal. You'll see there's a lot more here than meets the eye. Remember, according to the original report you gave my SOAR crew out at the Sturges's place, you saw a UFO hovering about the house. And Mowry reported seeing an alien being. Neither one of you are fantasy-prone individuals."

"I never said UFO. I said unknown craft."

"Exactly. Hal will tell you more about the scope of the operation when you get down there. You won't be in this alone. Should you need to call on Mowry or any other COG operatives, they'll be available. And if they should need you—"

"I'll be there."

"Thank you," Macauley said. "Now go out and get the story, Striker. And get that son of a bitch Goddard before he pulls off his mission."

THE CAR MACAULEY HAD waiting for the Executioner was actually a white Range Rover 4.6 HSE. It was outfitted with a roof rack full of strapped-down camping gear, a high-tech mountain-climbing suspension system and a dashboard computer.

According to the insurance and identification cards in the glove compartment, the Rover was registered in the name of his current alias, Gordon J. Miller.

It was the kind of vehicle a roving reporter like Miller could live out of as he trekked across the highways and the rugged desert passes of the Southwest. The off-road vehicle also had several other COG modifications that enhanced Bolan's chances of survival.

The sturdy vehicle would get him through a flash flood or a firefight.

Bolan drove south down Interstate 25, making good time in the sparse early-morning traffic. He rode parallel with the Rio Grande and stayed on the interstate all the way down past Socorro and through the quixotically named town of Truth or Consequences before heading west on Route 152.

Following the on-screen map display generated by Macauley's disk, he took a series of gravel and rough dirt roads that made it clear why they'd issued the Range Rover to him for the trip.

At the end of the last road was a gated complex of three long white buildings that seemed like totally functional blockhouses.

In the back of the buildings there was a wide stretch of flat land that led up to a gravel pit with a steep gouged-out slope. Several dark mounds of shale were perched on the edge of the escarpment. Close to the pit was a hangar-like garage that sheltered the bulldozers and utility trucks from the sun.

Brognola's latest digs almost looked like a real mining company, Bolan thought as he rolled to a stop just before the gate.

There was a wooden placard bolted on one side of the gate— Southwest Quarry Company. But the man who stepped out of the guard shack said otherwise.

He kept one hand close to his side arm at all times. The bill of his desert camo cap shadowed his dark sunglasses and gave no hint of the hard eyes behind the lenses.

"Turn off the engine," he said.

Bolan switched off the key.

"Take the key out of the ignition."

Bolan looked up, wondering if he had a bored guard who was hotdogging the situation because the only thing that passed this way was an occasional roadrunner or prairie dog. But Bolan gave him the benefit of the doubt. Just a serious guy doing his job and doing it in such a way that there could be no surprises.

Bolan took the key out of the ignition.

The guard leaned close to the driver's window, holding his left hand out and sweeping it left and right, as if he was divining the contents of the Range Rover. It appeared to be a lazy, natural motion. But it accomplished two things. First, it blocked Bolan from reaching out toward the guard. Second, it distracted Bolan's eyes and kept him from focusing on the hand that hovered near the side arm. Almost.

The laminated name tag across the guard's shirt pocket read S. Tilston.

Tilston bent close to the windows of the Rover as he walked all around it, looking for contraband or maybe little green aliens. It was hard to say. He took his time, making a slow circuit of the vehicle until he came back to the driver's side.

"Name?" Tilston said, looking at his clipboard.

"Miller," Bolan said. "Gordon J. Here to see Hal Brognola. I'm expected."

"We'll see," the guard said. "Look over there." He pointed at a video camera mounted on the windowsill of the shack.

Bolan glanced at the camera.

The guard went back into the shack and stayed there long enough for someone inside the complex to view the security video.

When he came back to the car he was a changed man. The aura of menace he'd cultivated was gone. Instead there was an almost friendly demeanor about him.

He lifted his tinted glasses and nodded at Bolan. "Welcome to the quarry, Mr. Miller," he said. "You can go through now. Next time we won't be so formal, now that I know who you are."

"I feel like I've known you all my life," Bolan said.

Tilston laughed and rapped the side of the Rover. Then he stepped back into the guard shack and opened the gates.

Bolan drove through the gates as they whirred inward and cruised toward the first building. Two other cars were parked by the solitary entrance to the building, a dark-tinted glass door at the back of a recessed alcove.

Hal Brognola stepped out from the entrance before Bolan was out of the Range Rover.

"Good to see you, Striker," he said, shaking his hand and clasping his shoulder. "Thanks for coming down so soon."

Bolan shrugged and looked around the stark surroundings. "How could I pass up a visit to this spa."

"It gets better," Brognola said. "Come inside."

The soldier stretched his long frame to shake off the effects of several hours of driving, then followed the big Fed through the glass door into the cool air-conditioned building.

The hallway opened into a modern lobby that was lined with smooth granite and soft recessed lighting that gave it a soothing atmosphere. A place sealed off from the outside world where some serious thinking could get done.

A large unmanned reception desk sat in the middle of the room with enough chairs for three people to man the desk.

The quarry was currently operating with a skeleton staff, but there was no shortage of space in case Brognola had to call in the troops. An open stairwell led down to at least one basement level and possibly several additional sublevels.

They took the stairs up to a second floor that was lined with offices, conference rooms and a break room.

Brognola led him into a small office that was alive with the hum of electrical equipment and a steady air-conditioned hiss. It looked like a control room. A bank of computers and communication gear was built into a console by the wall. Everything was switched on, ready to be called into action.

Just above the console was a thick panel of tinted Plexiglas that looked out onto the yard. There was a ceramic coffee mug, two empty mineral water bottles and crumpled wrappers from three or more candy bars. Fuel that kept Brognola going.

From past experience the Executioner figured Brognola had worked through the night in this desert command post, fielding teams against UFORCE and figuring out the next move that Goddard would make.

Close by the door was a small round table with three cushioned chairs. Bolan dropped into the nearest one, leaned it against the wall, and rested his elbow on the table. "Who goes first?" he asked.

"I'll start," Brognola said. "We've got a lot of ground to cover. Good thing you're sitting down, Striker."

"Why's that?"

"A strange report just came in from Albuquerque right before you got here. It's about the men you and Mowry took out."

"And?"

"They're all dead."

Bolan gave him a look. "Yeah, I know," he said. "I was there, Hal. I saw it."

"I mean they were dead before they even got to Sturges's place. They were also listed as dead. Every last one of them had previously been reported as missing in action, or else they were killed in training accidents where no body was recovered. Some of them were even buried with honors. Who knows what was in the coffins."

"Lot of trouble to go through," Bolan said.

"Not if it's your stock-in-trade," Brognola said. "They were obviously recruited for Colonel Goddard's covert strike teams. As part of his deniable-force philosophy, he made it appear as if they were long dead."

"What theater did they come from?" Bolan asked.

"Grenada, Panama, the Gulf, the Balkans, even right here in the States," Brognola said. "Fingerprints and DNA proved who they were."

"A dead brigade," Bolan said. "Phantom names for a phantom army."

The red-eyed Justice Department chief sighed and slowly nodded his head. "Afraid so," he said. "If he's got any more units like this, we won't know how many troops we're facing. That was always the problem with UFORCE. There was no way to rein it in once it got off the ground. We knew from the beginning that it could happen…"

The Executioner sat back and listened as Brognola filled him in on the origin of UFORCE.

It was originally designated simply as UFOR, typical military jargon for Unknown Force. Its mission statement was to create a deniable strike force for rapid insertion into conflict zones to wreak havoc on the target and obliterate any sign of its presence. Just in case word of the operation leaked out, UFOR always had a squad of spin doctors on the scene to cover its tracks. If necessary, disinformation campaigns or outright hoaxes were launched.

In its early stages the unit had several victories that won it the backing of Washington power brokers and Pentagon chiefs. More resources and manpower were channeled its way. Soon UFOR was supporting operations across the globe, drawing more and more black-budget funds into its orbit.

Goddard had also began working closely with the massive Continuity of Government covert apparatus, which had quietly built up underground shelters all across the country. The shelters were stocked with long-range provisions in the event COG had to haul the leadership underground during natural or military disasters. An alternate government body had been created to guide the country in case the leadership was wiped out.

Senators and congressmen and cabinet members all had their opposite numbers in COG who were ready to step in and fill their shoes during an emergency. There were even alternate president and vice president designees to grab the reins of power.

This was the famous shadow government that was often mistakenly talked about in the conspiracy press. Several articles had been written about "the Doubles," a group of secretly groomed duplicates who were planning on usurping power from the legitimate government. Some conspiracy journals said that it had already happened, that it was a fait accompli.

But the secret government was simply a fail-safe device to ensure that chaos and anarchy didn't supplant the legal government of the United States.

COG and UFOR managed to stay secret while growing beyond all expectations.

When the first prototype stealth crafts rolled off the line, some of them were naturally provided to Goddard's UFOR operation. A considerable amount of weaponry developed for the Army's Defense Advanced Research Projects Agency—or DARPA—also found its way into Goddard's armory.

Goddard started to take on more and more missions, setting up off-the-shelf covert strike forces and front companies to separate his operations from the U.S. government. His plainclothes "civilian" units infiltrated several classified research projects and channeled their assets into his covert kingdom.

Gradually Goddard led the unit in directions few men dared to anticipate. With the stealth craft and psy-war operatives at his beck and call, he began to mask his operations with UFO-like activity. The unit evolved into UFORCE, a stealth unit that crossed borders unseen. It could take out hostile leaders or run a psy-ops number on them to make them look like raving lunatics to the rest of the world.

When some UFORCE psy-war op turned out badly, leaving State Department honchos to patch up the bloody messes Goddard left behind, Washington called for a halt to the UFO angle. Goddard complied. On the surface. In reality he went deep black and took UFORCE to even greater extremes.

Instead of just creating the illusion that UFOs were flying in the skies, he had created an "alien unit' to convince his targets they were dealing with an extraterrestrial force. Rumors circulated that UFORCE was engaged in abductions, mind-control operations, mutilations and murder. Some rumors said that he actually was in league with alien intelligences that had infiltrated the U.S. government.

"As crazy as it sounds, no one really believed he was doing

it at first," Brognola said. "After all, UFO sightings have been with us since the forties. Abductions and weird genetic experimentations were a staple of pop culture in the fifties and sixties right up to the present day."

"And no one wanted to believe that UFORCE was behind it," Bolan stated.

"But we should have," Brognola said. "There were more than enough warning signs. We just didn't take them seriously. That changed when we began to get reports of unusual sightings in Mexico and Colombia that were accompanied by violent acts— a new wrinkle in the UFO mythology. These military-style encounters occurred up and down the Central American drug pipeline. Many of the cartel leaders were hit and their drug armies destroyed."

"Wasn't that one of the goals of UFORCE?" Bolan said. "Sounds like they achieved it."

"Temporarily," Brognola replied. "But a newer and more sophisticated breed filled the vacuum."

"They always do," the Executioner stated.

"Exactly," Brognola said. "But our main concern was that the drugs and cash seized from the cartels ended up in Goddard's hands. All signs pointed toward him, but nothing could be proven. How could it? We had a covert-ops group that could conduct operations outside of our border totally unnoticed. Before we knew it, he began conducting them *inside* our borders."

The Executioner nodded. "Yeah, I saw that firsthand," he said, remembering the craft hovering above Sturges's house and how it had so quietly dropped its hit team onto the roof. "A lethal force with a mind-bending delivery system. Good thing to have in our arsenal. But why did he turn rogue?"

"Because he was a righteous man," Brognola said. "Or thought he was. In his view he was the frontline defense of the country. All of a sudden these narrow-minded bureaucrats were going to shut him down."

Brognola paused long enough to take a drink of coffee.

"So he started planning for the day he had to take his operation underground,'' Brognola continued. "Along with diverting black-budget resources, he developed alternate sources of funding. Cartels. Corrupt foreign leaders. It's all right there.''

Brognola pointed at the bank of computers. "He had a lot of friends in Washington, so we needed ironclad proof of his guilt. We started gathering files that directly tied the illegal activities to Goddard himself. We were about to close him down for good when someone in the GAO jumped the gun, unaware of the parallel work we were doing. They sent one of their top investigators on a site visit to Gideon. He went in, and as you know, he never came out.''

"Taylor," Bolan said. "The first disappearance.''

"The first one we knew of,'' Brognola replied. "There were several others. Goddard knew this was coming. We can tell by what he left behind at his Gideon operation.''

"Files?'' Bolan said.

"Some hard drives were salvaged from Gideon. Some hardcopy files, too.''

"What's on them?''

"Names,'' Brognola said. "Hundreds of names. Lists of collaborators. Lists of targets marked for dirty tricks. Reporters. Mercenaries. Media syndicates. Employment records of people who supposedly worked for him.''

"Sounds like a gold mine.''

"Yeah. Mostly fool's gold. I think Goddard's muddying the waters with bogus information. He knew we could track some of his people. By providing us with a list of both friends and enemies, he's tying up a lot of our resources. He knows we'll have to check and double-check all of his lists to see what's real and what's disinformation. Meanwhile, Macauley and I are creating some lists of our own.''

"More targets like Sturges?''

"Right," Brognola said. "And a list of possible collaborators, like the ones who helped him shoot down the Hercules.''

Bolan saw the pain in Brognola's face. Pain that came from the loss of good men and the knowledge that more sacrifices lay ahead. Goddard had declared war on the United States, a high-tech guerrilla war that was only going to escalate. "Know whether it was sabotage yet?"

"No. The verdict's still out. But whether it was sabotage or a shoot down, Goddard had a hand in it."

"He'll pay," Bolan promised.

"First we have to find him," Brognola said. "Right now our best leads will come from identifying Goddard's collaborators. Or if we capture one of his people when they move against their next targets."

"I know that was the game plan for me and Mowry, Hal," the Executioner said. "Sorry it didn't work out."

"In a way it did," Brognola replied. "You drew blood and you forced him to withdraw from the field."

"It was luck," Bolan said. "Goddard's crew didn't expect to encounter armed resistance that night, and he didn't know what kind of force we had waiting in reserve."

The Executioner flashed back to the aftermath of the sudden battle. It had been a close call for Goddard. His skirmish force almost walked into a full-scale engagement. Commander Macauley's SOAR choppers arrived shortly after the attack on Mowry's position. By then UFORCE was gone. The craft had fled and the ground team was wiped out.

"Call it luck if you want," Brognola said. "The fact remains that he was still driven from the field. That should shake some of his people. Until now they believed he was invincible."

The big Fed finished briefing the Executioner on the evolution of UFORCE, then walked over to a file cabinet next to his desk.

"All right," Brognola said, opening up the bottom drawer. "That was the rise of UFORCE. Now let's start planning its downfall." He withdrew a thick file that had about ten pounds of confidential documents stuffed inside. As soon as he placed it on the table, several of the documents slid out.

"What are these?"

"Some background for your cover identity," Brognola said.

"Goddard cloaks his operations in UFO activity because it matches the kind of trail he leaves behind. That trail's occasionally picked up by UFO enthusiasts, witnesses, hard-core researchers and military and law-enforcement assets who file reports."

"And it's all in here?" Bolan said, resting his arm on the thick stack of documents.

"You wish," Brognola said. "That's only a fraction of what's available. The government has libraries full of the stuff, not even counting the computer files. But that should get you started."

"And when I need a break, I'll just start lifting weights," Bolan said, hoisting the heavy file up and down before dropping it on the table with a big thud.

Brognola laughed. "Sorry to hit you with so much all at once, Striker. But you have to learn the personalities and jargon. We've got people in place in the UFO field. So does Goddard. The more you know, the better your chances of staying alive."

"About this cover, Hal."

"It's not the usual gig, is it?"

Bolan shook his head. "It's pretty far out there."

"Wait'll you see what's inside," Brognola said, rapping the stack of files. "After you go through them, we'll talk."

THREE HOURS and several cups of coffee later, Bolan pushed the files aside.

He was sitting at a long table in the break room. Papers were spread across the surface as if he were doing a year's worth of homework in one sitting. The documents, dossiers and background papers provided him with a glimpse of a world that he'd never fully explored.

It wasn't the world of UFOs and aliens that surprised him. It was the subculture that sprang up around it. A world inhabited by researchers and psychiatrists, scientists and true believers, experiencers and celebrity abductees. There were a lot of serious people involved along with the hoaxers, tabloid hacks and some psychologically disturbed individuals.

Over the past two decades the fringe phenomenon had almost become mainstream. The cosmic awakening had become an unstoppable growth industry.

With his head full of a brave new world to digest, Bolan got up and took a walk around the second floor.

Even with its state-of-the-art offices and conference rooms, it was hard to disguise the fact that the building was a hardsite designed to withstand a serious attack. He wondered how long Brognola would stay here before Goddard moved against him.

On his second circuit of the floor, the Executioner saw Brognola stepping out of his office into the long carpeted corridor. He caught up with him and walked toward a corner area that looked out onto the quarry.

"What do you think so far?" Brognola asked.

The Executioner shrugged. "I've got a lot more to learn if I'm going to pull off this cover bit."

"It'll come," Brognola said. "We'll have people help you along the way."

"Whose idea was it, Hal? Commander Macauley said it was yours."

"Guilty."

"That's reassuring."

"Why?"

"If it was Macauley's idea, I'd suspect it was a way to keep tabs on me—and keep me away from the real action."

"I can see how it'd look that way," Brognola said. "But you've got nothing to worry about."

"Maybe," Bolan stated. "What about the beacon he planted in the Range Rover?"

"You mean the global positioning system? GPS is standard issue these days."

"No," Bolan said. "I mean the hidden transmitter I found in the travel rack when I pulled over in a rest area to check it out. I left it in place for now. It was a bit of a shock to find it."

"Hey, rental companies do the same thing," Brognola said. "He's a cautious man. Maybe even a bit of a control freak. But I don't see any dark design in it. And it sounds like something you and I would do under similar circumstances."

"So Macauley's beyond suspicion?"

Brognola thought long and hard. The typical response would be to give an immediate and unqualified yes. No one liked to be questioned about their allies. But both of their lives were on the line so he weighed it carefully before he answered.

"Yes," Brognola said. "Macauley is beyond suspicion. For one thing he and I go back a ways. Besides, if he was in league with UFORCE, then neither of us would be alive right now. He's like us, Striker. He doesn't dance around. He goes straight for the kill."

The Executioner nodded. He had faith in Brognola's judgment. But at times like this a little paranoia was a healthy thing.

He still didn't like the idea that Macauley knew exactly where both of them were at all times. The Quarry command post was his. So was the Range Rover. He probably had a few other means of surveillance in place.

"You on board with this, Striker?"

"Yeah, Hal. I'm in."

Brognola nodded. "Let's start thinking about your agenda. You make first contact tomorrow."

4

San Antonio, Texas

The dull, gray van rumbled down the alley and slowed just long enough for a man to slip out through the half-open sliding door.

Without looking around, he headed straight for the side entrance of the building that had been breached by the advance team. They'd also unscrewed the bulb from the caged light just over the entrance.

No one could see a thing.

He was inside before the van reached the end of the alley.

DR. WENDELL SCHYLER heard the groaning and clacking of the forty-nine-year-old elevator as it made its way up to the sixth floor of the Hartman Building.

He smiled. That was part of the charm of the seven-story professional building. It wasn't as sterile as the skyscrapers that towered over it in the heart of San Antonio's downtown district. It was an old and comfortable building with a lot of stonework, a lot of tradition and a lot of creaks.

As far as Schyler was concerned, he had the best of all possible worlds. Although the opposite side of the building was shadowed by modern high-rises, his side looked out toward the La Villita district with its nineteenth-century reconstructions of early San Antonio homes.

The building was a bridge between the old and the new world, and that made it the perfect location for this phase of his career. For five years now he'd been back in private practice, renewing his enthusiasm for his psychiatric work...and trying to regain the conscience he'd left behind in the secret corridors of the covert world.

Part of his mind followed the progress of the elevator, idly wondering who else was working at this time of night, but then he quickly lost himself in his work just as he did many nights before heading home to his wife. She alone understood how important it was to him. He already had wealth and a certain amount of fame in his field, but what he wanted most was redemption.

The tip of his fountain pen scratched across blue-lined notebook pages in a quick fluid motion as he wrote the extract for one of the psychiatric cases he planned to include in his second book.

The *San Antonio Times* had called his first book "a terrifying yet often whimsical look at the heights and depths of the human mind." His second book would map out much deeper terrain. This time he was going to focus on screen memories, cult syndromes and the array of neuroses that faced alleged UFO abductees.

Although he was computer literate, Schyler still preferred to write with pen and paper. It gave him a more immediate connection to the patients he wrote about. When it came time to actually enter the text into his computer, he would of course change the names of his clients and add enough fictional details to protect their anonymity.

But the essential truth would come out. And hopefully this book would help others as much as the first. Judging by the volume of letters he received from readers of the first book, there were a lot of troubled souls out there looking for guidance. He felt obligated to provide it to them.

Wendell Schyler wanted to rebuild minds, not tear them down. That was why he wrote night after night, filling composition notebooks with accounts of the people who came to him for help. It purged the memory of the old days.

A rattling sound from his outer office yanked Schyler's attention away from the notebook.

Someone was turning the heavy brass handle.

He capped the fountain pen and eased his chair away from the desk. Then he quietly crossed the room and looked into the outer office.

It was dead quiet now. Whoever it was had probably gone away. But still… He strode across the carpet, flipped the lock and pulled open the door.

The man who filled the doorway flashed him an easy smile.

"Hello, Doctor," the man said, opening his palm to reveal a cylindrical drill and lock pick. "I was hoping I didn't have to use this. Wasn't sure if you were here at first." He dropped it into the side pocket of his light brown business suit and inched his foot across the threshold.

"Who are you?" Schyler demanded, holding the door tight, ready to swing it shut.

"Colonel Goddard sent me."

The mention of Goddard's name sapped Schyler's resistance. He numbly stepped aside as the man walked into the room and closed the door behind him. "It's about the UFORCE project you worked on."

"UFORCE?"

"Surely you remember the name?"

"Yes," Schyler said. "Of course. But I don't remember you." He studied the man's face. Well-trimmed brown mustache, strong jaw and impressive physique.

"The name is Stevenson. Captain Stevenson. I worked at many of the same facilities as you, but usually behind the scenes."

"I'm afraid I don't remember too much about those days."

"Good, good," Stevenson enthused. "Selective memory's important in this business."

"I'm out of the business forever. Washed my hands of it."

Stevenson nodded. "That should make my visit a lot simpler." The tall man looked toward Schyler's office. The inner sanctum. "Shall we go in there?"

It wasn't a request. This man got what he wanted through force of will or force of arms. Schyler led him into the room.

Stevenson immediately went to the desk and peered at the notebook, turning it so he could decipher the handwriting.

"That's private," Schyler said, closing the book and sliding it back toward his side of the desk.

The tall man shrugged. "Sit down, Dr. Schyler. Let's talk."

Stevenson remained on his feet and paced in front of the desk.

"What's this about?" Schyler asked.

"Unfortunately the UFORCE protocols have changed. We've been forced to go underground and sever all ties to the government."

Dr. Schyler couldn't hide his shock. It was like saying one part of the country had seceded from the other. "Why?"

"Never mind the details," Stevenson said. "All you need to know is that our entire operation is being scrutinized by a group of Washington headhunters. Sooner or later anyone connected to the project will be interrogated."

"My work was secret," Schyler protested. "The funding came from university grants and—"

"It doesn't matter. These people know all about those shell games. Eventually they'll find you. We've got to be prepared for that. Get our stories straight about the alien thing."

"They were hypothetical scenarios."

Stevenson smiled. "You weren't paid that kind of money for hypotheticals, Doctor. Everything you developed for us— the visitation scenario, the drugs, the abductions, mutilations, alien hieroglyphics and revelations—was put into practice. Particularly the harassment techniques. Extremely effective."

As Schyler looked up at Colonel Goddard's emissary, all of the work he'd done for UFORCE came back to him.

"And of course there was the matter of the experimental subjects," Stevenson continued. "The things that were done to them were highly irregular."

"They were volunteers who knew the risks," Schyler said.

"Were they?" Stevenson shrugged. "I think we all knew otherwise."

They'd led him down the path step by step. At first he simply followed along, but then he got caught up in the project and forged ahead of them all, always looking for a way to extend the boundaries. He was part of the grand secret. A member of a powerful fraternity with unlimited resources. How could he resist?

Schyler had begun with real-world reports of UFO sightings and encounters. Then he added esoteric elements to the mix.

Jungian concepts of UFO archetypes and religious impulses.

Drug-induced states.

Implants to track subjects and alter brain-wave patterns.

And then there was EDOM, the technique that was as ominous as it sounded. Electronic Dissolution of Memory was a method used on "abductees" to erase memories of their real encounters and plant false memories in their place. He'd taken ideas that were initially developed to expand knowledge of human consciousness and turned them into weapons.

And then of course there was the disinformation agency he helped to create. The silencers, the shadow agents, the MIB. They were known by several different names, but their purpose was the same. Sow the seeds of hysteria. Intimidate witnesses, create the illusion otherworldly forces were at work.

And that was just *his* work. Schyler was only one of many researchers working for a highly compartmentalized psy-war project. Who knew what the others came up with? Initially they all convinced themselves that research in itself was harmless. But even back then Schyler knew that any time someone developed a weapon, he found a reason to use it.

"Makes you think, doesn't it?" Stevenson said. "If any of this gets out…"

"I understand," Schyler said. He was resigned to the need for a cover-up. Otherwise he would be throwing away everything he'd worked for during these past five years. "What do you want from me?"

"Just one thing to start with," Stevenson replied. "The

truth." He rested his hands on the desk and leaned toward him, boring his eyes into his. "Who else knows about the work you did for us?"

Schyler hesitated a moment too long before answering. "No one." he said weakly.

And in that instant Stevenson knew he was lying. In that same instant Schyler knew he was about to be killed. *After* UFORCE used the treatments on him. Treatments he helped develop.

Schyler snatched the phone off his desk, surprising himself and Stevenson with his speed. In one continuous move he spun around and bashed the heavy base of the phone against the window. The bottom panel of glass shattered just below the latch.

He struck the top window before Stevenson dived toward the window and clutched at Schyler's hand just as the glass shattered.

But the damage was done. The phone hurtled to the street below in a shower of glass. And Wendell Schyler's scream was echoing over the rooftops.

The scream was full of rage and victory all at once. He knew he was finished, but at least they couldn't make it look like an accident now. Someone would hear; someone would come to investigate. And his wife would be warned.

Schyler's back exploded with a nova of pain that spread through his body. He arched his back by reflex but still managed to hold on to the glass-sprinkled crossbar of the window frame.

Stevenson drove his granite knuckles into the small of his back again and clawed his fingers deep into Schyler's scalp. He yanked back on his hair, starting to pry him away from the window. "Now we have a different kind of talk," he promised.

Schyler grabbed at the iron window latch so hard that it broke off into his hand. The sudden release propelled both of them back into the room. As he started to fall backward, Schyler slashed the jagged handle behind him.

It sunk home. Briefly.

And then he was falling in the air.

Schyler landed flat on his back just in time to see blood spatter from a long gash on the other man's neck. It ran from just under his ear down to his collarbone and had narrowly missed his throat.

The UFORCE captain bellowed in pain and clasped one hand to the deep wound. Rivulets of blood seeped through his fingers as he stood over Schyler.

And then Schyler saw the twisted face hovering above him. Gone was the facade of the perfectly controlled man. The raging killer who slept behind the pleasant mask emerged. The operation had gone wrong. So had his thoughts. Unable to think straight, enraged that such a puny man had caused him an almost fatal wound, Stevenson shot his callused palm straight down at the fallen doctor.

It crushed his forehead like an eggshell.

As the crack of breaking cartilage cchoed through his skull, Schyler wondered if he would feel any pain. Then he suddenly stopped wondering anything at all.

"GET UP HERE NOW."

The driver of the escape van was surprised to hear Captain Stevenson's voice on the dashboard transceiver.

"Can't do it," the driver said. "Too much noise. Cops'll be on the way soon."

"Then we'll take them the fuck out. Hurry up. I'm cut and we got to haul some things out of here."

The driver looked over at the man in the passenger seat. Dark glasses. Dark future for anyone who got in his way. "You heard him, Chet," the other man said. "We've got no choice."

When have we ever? Chet Matthews thought. When the colonel said to do something, you did it or died trying. He'd help you either way.

Matthews shifted the van into gear and rolled down the street. He turned down the alley once more and headed toward the side entrance. When he was just about even with the entrance, he tapped on the brake and swung the wheel sharply to the left, parking the van at an angle so nothing could get past them and hem them in.

Then he grabbed the Heckler & Koch submachine gun from the rack behind the back seat. He checked the magazine, then followed the other man inside the Hartman Building, wondering what kind of cleanup awaited them.

BROKEN WINDOWS on the top floor. Patrol car in the alley, bubble top flashing its lights behind a gray van wedged in the driveway.

It didn't take a news anchor to realize there was a story here. Not that Janice Regan was the type who would ever sit behind a desk, or even want to. She had the figure, but not the right face. Attractive but alternative. High cheekbones, spiky hair.

She was a stringer, a video guerrilla who sold her clips to stations all across the Southwest, now and then striking it rich by placing a piece with the networks. She drifted from natural disasters like floods and hurricanes to human disasters like police standoffs and homicides, going wherever her police scanners would take her.

That was why she was now crouched at the far end of the alley peering through a night-vision video camera that still had Property Of WMDZ engraved upon it. WMDZ was a station back east that had burned her on a piece one of their producers repackaged for the networks. She returned the favor by walking off with one of their cameras.

The state-of-the-art camera had served her well, helping her bring to light news that otherwise might never see broadcast.

Regan zoomed in on the steps near the entrance where one uniformed officer was standing by the railing at the bottom of the steps. He kept his hand near his holster, taking his backup role seriously.

Another officer stood on the platform by the partially open door, talking to an extremely tall man who was showing him some kind of ID. The tall man also had some kind of bandage on his neck.

Whatever happened was over with, and this was the guy who put an end to it. He said something to the officer that relaxed him a bit. The cop obviously wasn't too pleased at what he was hearing but he was no longer on alert. Instead of running into a potentially hostile situation, the only fight the officer had on his hand was a battle over turf.

She'd been around enough police actions to know there was always a pissing contest to see who was top dog on the scene.

This time around it was obviously the tall guy. Must be some kind of spook or high-ranking plainclothes detective, Regan thought. That was good news for her. If someone of that caliber was involved, then she might have a story on her hands. She never knew where these things could lead.

Unfortunately a lot of the story would have to be guesswork. She couldn't hear what they were saying because the video camera, though excellent for visuals under just about any light conditions, had a limited range for pulling in voices.

Regan wished she had her long-range directional mike, but that was in the back of her battered news mobile, a bullet-nosed van that was probably still circling the neighborhood somewhere.

The man who was driving the van for her was Lazarus Erasque, an out-of-work sound engineer and voice-over talent she hung with whenever she hit San Antonio.

When he'd seen the back of the alley blocked by the patrol car and van, he wheeled down a side street and then circled back to drop her off near La Villita so she could approach from that direction unseen.

Regan moved the camera slightly when she saw additional movement in the doorway. A second man stood there. And then a third. They were carrying satchels. And one of them held a handful of files.

Evidence? Theft? Had to be something explosive to make them go to all this trouble, she thought. Someone didn't transfer files in the middle of the night unless he wanted to keep it secret.

But somewhere along the way they'd screwed up, and it was up to her to find out where.

The tall man put his arm around the shoulder of the officer and guided him away from the door and down the steps toward the patrol car.

That's when the argument started. Apparently the plain-clothes man wanted the cops to leave, but they were just as determined to stay.

So the cop wasn't rolling over after all. Another car was probably on the way. Maybe there'd be a showdown between the uniforms and the plainclothes team.

And then she thought she was seeing things. The tall man turned his back on the cops and made a hand signal that only his men—and Janice Regan—could see.

He was giving them the thumbs-down.

Bright spear-point flashes erupted from beneath the satchels, and the rattle of automatic gunfire echoed down the alley.

The sudden volley ripped into the cops before either of them knew what was happening. The one who'd been arguing with the tall man crumpled to the ground and curled into a fetal position.

The other officer had been knocked steadily backward as the bullets drilled into him. He collapsed against the patrol car but managed to unholster his weapon and fire one wild shot at his ambushers.

Both gunmen stepped forward and hosed down the alley like exterminators. The bullets spun the officer around and dropped him face first in the alley.

Regan didn't realize she'd screamed until she saw the tall man looking her way. Even so she kept right on taping as she backed away from him. Then when she saw his hand reaching inside his jacket, she turned and ran.

Thank God she hadn't been any closer, she thought as she beat a retreat across a courtyard. She ran straight for a wooden fence, slammed her hand down on the slats for leverage, and then vaulted over it. While she was in the air she knew she'd never be able to do something like that again. Nor would she want to.

Something crashed into the fence. She heard the sound of splintering wood and the ricochet of bullets skipping down the street.

The bastard was shooting at her!

She kept on running without looking behind. To do so would slow her just enough to catch a bullet.

From somewhere behind her, she heard the man's feet skidding on the dry pavement when he came to a stop.

Then she heard the sirens coming. He couldn't afford to risk a wild chase through unknown territory while other patrol cars were on the way.

Regan's heart thumped crazily as she pumped her arms like a championship runner, gripping tightly to the video camera every step of the way.

She stepped out onto the street, heard a screech of tires and then saw a pair of headlights crashing down on her.

She covered her face with the camera and vaguely saw someone's head poking out of the driver's window.

"Come on, get in, get in."

It was Lazarus Erasque.

"Thank God it's you," she shouted. She ran to the side of the van just as he flung open the door. She hopped into the passenger seat and slammed the door, looked behind her as they sped down the street.

"Don't worry," he said. "This is my town. They won't find us."

She looked over at the freelance sound man, who had to be as scared as she was. But he was grinning brightly as he floored the van around another corner.

"What are you so happy about, Laz?" she asked, pinned to the seat by the acceleration.

"We're alive," he said. "You can't ask for much more than that."

Regan laughed, still riding high on adrenaline herself. "No," she said. "Guess not." She gave herself a half minute to let her heart rate slow to normal before she spoke again. "You saw what happened?"

He shook his head. "Not all of it. But I sure as hell heard it. I was just about to walk around the corner when the shooting started. Just caught a glimpse of what was going down, enough to know it was time to be scarce."

He gestured at the video camera she was still gripping tightly.

"What about you? Did you catch it all?"

"Pretty much," she said. "Got the shooters and I got the tall man."

"The who?"

"The guy behind it all. When you see those eyes looking your way, you won't forget him. Especially when he's planning to kill you."

He instinctively looked in the side mirror of the van. "Nothing," he said. "We lost him."

She shook her head and exhaled. "Maybe," she said. "But I don't think we're going to see this guy until it's too late. One second you're there—the next you're gone. That's his style. Wait until you see the tape and you'll see what I mean."

Erasque stopped at a red light, saw a parking spot by a Mexican restaurant, then backed into it and shut off the lights.

"What are you doing?" Regan asked.

He switched off the engine. "I'm thinking. We haven't done that since we hauled ass away from there. We got to figure out our next move."

"Yeah," she said. "You're right."

"So?" He tapped the video camera. "Who do we sell it to?"

She touched his wrist and clenched it tight. "I'm thinking we might not sell it, Laz. I'm thinking that might be the worst thing we could do."

His eyes looked at her as if she were a stranger. They'd been friends, lovers and friends again. Trust had built up between them over the years, but she wasn't sure if it could stand up to the lure of money.

"That's one plan," he said. "But if you're thinking that way, then we're in the wrong business. Come on, babe, you can't sit on something like this."

She looked at the camera that held their future. On one hand it made a lot of sense to sell it and go public. Sic the authorities on the killers she caught in the act. But that only made sense if she believed the guy on tape wouldn't come after her for exposing him.

"We'll decide together," she said. "Let's go to your place, make some dubs and take a hard look at what we got."

"I know what we got already," he said. "That kind of footage is enough to make us a little bit rich."

"Yeah," she said. "Maybe even enough to pay for our funerals."

5

Black Wall, New Mexico

"TranceFormation" was one of the fastest-growing nationally syndicated radio shows in the country. The three-hour program covered the usual late-night subjects like UFOs, alien abductions, psychic warfare and secret technology hidden from the public. One of its most popular features was the *Conspiracy du Jour,* where leading researchers and regular listeners phoned in with updates on a chosen conspiracy.

But the show also explored more arcane areas like the secret of Rennes Le Chateau and its connection to the Grail family, and relics like the Spear of Longinus that pierced Christ on the cross and allegedly ended up in the hands of Hitler's Black Order. The show was basically a forum for whatever caught the fancy of Nicodemus Vril, the show's maverick host.

At the moment Vril was talking about golems and *tulpas,* the zombie-like thought forms or protoplasmic doubles that were created and controlled by human adepts. "Later in our show we'll hear from a man who not only claims to have met one of these thought forms but was able to create one himself. A practitioner of martial—and mental—arts, tonight's guest says he learned the technique from a Tibetan master he encountered while on assignment for the CIA, or as we are wont to call it, the Central Information Abyss. Where truth goes in and mythology comes out."

Bolan was listening to the broadcast from the Green Room of the Reality Base Radio Network, where guests could watch

Vril through the soundproof control-room window. The talk-show host's lyrical bass voice came from a corner speaker that also doubled as a bookshelf for several of his books.

Bolan got up and walked around the Green Room, which took about three seconds. It was little more than a couch and a coffee table covered with trade magazines that were spread across the surface like shingles.

From his briefing with Hal Brognola and the articles he'd read about Vril, Bolan knew why the Green Room was so cramped compared to the rest of the complex Vril grandly called the Reality Base Radio Network. Most of Vril's interviews were done over the phone, so there was little need to build a plush reception area. Just enough for a temporary landing space for occasional guests who trekked out to his western New Mexico outpost on the outskirts of the Gila National Forest.

Out here Nicodemus Vril had the plains in front of him and the wild ranges of the Tularosa Mountains behind him. To most natives of New Mexico, it was known as the high country where Apache warriors once made their home. But to the talk-show host, its main claim to fame was the tremendous number of UFO sightings along with unexplained military activity in the area. That was the lure that brought him out here from his East Coast arena and prompted him to set up shop here.

On top of the flat-roofed dwelling a garden of satellite dishes and antennae connected the radio station to the world at large. Everything he needed was at his fingertips. Transmitters beamed his show to syndicate-linked stations around the country, and his Internet connection provided him with tips and input from his nationwide fan base.

In case Vril ever ran out of supplies or needed human company, all he had to do was drive ten miles to the town of Black Wall, which owed its name to the lava bed north of town. The dark moonscape had a history of eerie sightings. Just about everyone in town had claimed to see strange spheres of light and ghostly apparitions above the lava beds. Every time Vril returned from Black Wall with a load of groceries, he also came back with fresh gossip and ghost stories.

Electronic trills and synthesized beats from a science-fiction soundtrack suddenly boomed from the speaker across from Bolan. The On The Air sign above the door flashed on, and Vril was back in action.

"We're back once again with 'TranceFormation,' your radio guide to the coming cosmic changes..."

Vril faded the music and went into one of his signature spiels. "An era of new beginnings, when we sleepers will finally wake to our purpose in the world. And find out once and for all whether we're part of God's grand plan, an alien experiment or merely a cosmic rash on the backside of the universe...

"Here to add another piece to the puzzle is our guest for the evening, a genuine secret agent who must remain nameless for the time being, calling in from Seattle, Washington, uh, make that Bar Harbor, Maine. Until he gives us permission otherwise, we'll simply refer to him as Agent X."

Bolan listened to the highly imaginative "agent" spin his tale about his encounter with thought forms. Agent X served up an intriguing confection that somehow involved Madame Blavatsky's secret masters, clandestine CIA technology and mental doppelgängers who could occasionally take on human form. The agent cautioned that someone could only create a strong thought form if his brain waves were tuned to the proper frequency.

The Executioner gave Vril a lot of credit. He let the guest play out his fantasy before gently probing with a few questions that wore away at the man's credibility but not his dignity.

Bolan sat back on the couch and fell into a trance state of his own. He'd been on the road for a while driving out here and he'd already sat through the first hour of the show, an open-line phantasmagoria where the callers talked about everything under the sun and beyond.

It wasn't the content of the show that surprised Bolan the most. It was the breadth of experience that the "Trance-

Formation'' host had behind him at such a relatively young age.

Nicodemus Vril was only in his midthirties, yet he was featured in national magazines, hosted and lectured at UFO conferences and was the sole owner of the Reality Base Radio Network. Along with "TranceFormation" he packaged other radio features beside his own—short bits of offbeat Americana sent in by correspondents from around the country that he sold to public radio stations and college radio.

Vril was truly a renaissance man of weird radio.

It took a while to turn a profit from "TranceFormation," but with Vril's contacts in the business and his accessible radio persona, it was inevitable that he would reach the big time. Another thing that helped his ascent in the field was his personal involvement in one of the most documented but least understood incidents in the history of modern UFO sightings.

Vril had been stationed at the Woodbridge Air Force Base in England during the Rendlesham Forest incident.

There, in a strip of forest between Woodbridge and the neighboring base at Bentwaters, a bona fide UFO had landed.

The craft had been seen by American and British base commanders, as well as security personnel and several local inhabitants. There were tape recordings of senior officers from both bases as they reported their real-time encounter with a shape-changing disk that they chased through the woods.

At first it appeared to be two brilliant spheres of light pinwheeling through the sky. Then it took on a triangular shape with flashing lights. It landed in the forest, close enough to touch, and left behind impressions on the ground.

A number of witnesses reported strange sensations as they neared the object. Nausea. Altered states of consciousness. Strange humming sounds in their ears. One of the witnesses was Second Lieutenant Nicodemus Virilosa, who was serving as public-information officer at the time.

He arrived in the middle of the Rendlesham woods shortly after the security teams and senior officers formed a half circle

around the object. Other teams were circling around the woods
to cordon off the area.

He saw the craft, felt some kind of frontal lobe stimulation,
and then saw it blink out of existence. Just like that it was
gone, and all of them were staring into the dark empty space
where moments ago it had been a concrete object.

He'd been obsessed with the incident ever since and was
still trying to figure out what had really happened that night.
Despite all of the books and documentaries that came out about
it, no one on the base knew anything about the ship. No one
off the base knew, either, though they certainly flooded the
media with their speculations.

Vril believed the real story hadn't been told—not because
the Air Force was covering it up—but because the operators
of the craft were conducting a test on one of its most sophisticated targets. If the Air Force couldn't figure out what was
going on, who could?

In his mind there was only one answer. Nicodemus Vril. For
the rest of his Air Force tour he used his position as information officer to gather up every bit of evidence he could.

It wasn't enough.

He continued digging into the story after he got out of the
service and went into the broadcasting business, shortening his
radio name to Vril along the way.

He wrote about the incident in his newsletter, in magazine
articles, and he sifted material sent to him by fans and fellow
researchers. But he was never in a position to uncover the
story.

Until now, Bolan thought.

The unexplained phenomenon behind the Rendlesham sighting and the UFORCE operation might be one and the same
thing.

This could be the trade-off that won Vril's cooperation. In
return for guiding Bolan through the UFO underworld, he
could get the story once and for all.

If they all lived through it, Bolan thought.

He glanced through the window again and saw Vril gesturing with his hands as he spoke, chopping the air whenever he made a point, or spreading his hands in front of him, palms up, whenever he posed a question to the audience.

Vril still had a military look about him. His short hair had grown out just enough to show its black color. He wore faded jeans and a gray sweatshirt with sleeves rolled up to the elbows, showing the forearms of a man who kept in shape.

There were no airs about him. Just a man who wanted to get the job done, even if that job was finding the secrets of the universe.

About ten minutes later, Vril announced that after the next set of commercials he was going to play a taped interview sent in by one of his frequent correspondents. He flicked on the control-board switch that ran the automated tape sequence, then stepped out into the Green Room.

"There," Vril said, nodding back at the control room. "That should give us some time. Sorry to keep you waiting so long."

"No problem," Bolan replied. "I appreciate the chance to see you work. Get an idea of what you do out here."

"It beats working for a living," he said.

Bolan laughed, knowing that the man never really stopped working. And his work was going to get a lot harder in the near future.

"Now, what is it you wanted to discuss?" Vril asked. "You come highly recommended from our mutual friend in Washington. But I must confess, he was rather vague on the phone about your reasons for wanting to come out here."

"He was vague for a reason," Bolan said. "It's not the kind of thing you like to talk about on unprotected lines."

"Don't I know it! NSA's Project Echelon monitors every phone call, e-mail, fax, satellite transmission, you can take your pick. And it's all routed through their decoding center at Fort Meade. Though you're relatively new to the field, you probably know something about it, don't you?"

"Somewhat," Bolan said, though he knew more than most. He was also aware that Vril was fencing with him again, just as he'd done when Bolan arrived shortly before his show went on the air. He was trying to find out where his visitor stood and measure his response. The man had a built-in lie detector. "It's done some good," Bolan said. "Despite what everyone says."

Several of Brognola's sensitive operations benefited from the intelligence-gathering capacities of Echelon. By using a vacuum technique that seized on key words in communications traffic, Project Echelon often exposed terrorist actions before they could be carried out. It also helped the covert community track down hostile targets.

"Don't tell me you're in favor of such widespread snooping?" Vril asked.

Bolan shrugged. "It's just a tool," he replied. "Like everything else, there's a chance for abuse. But it's not really a threat to the average person. These days everyone is sophisticated enough to realize no communications are safe from eavesdropping. Except for face-to-face like this."

"I wonder," Vril said, looking at Bolan with an impish smile. "Do you think there's a chance someone from the government might be listening to us as we speak?"

Bolan laughed it off. Obviously Vril thought he worked for the government. But then, again, in the UFO subculture it wasn't such a wild thought.

"Back to our friend and the reason for your visit," Vril said.

The "TranceFormation" host started talking about their supposed mutual friend in Washington. The man's name was David Arthur. Everything Bolan knew about him came from his briefing with Brognola.

David Arthur was one of Vril's "inside sources," and they'd known each other since their Air Force days. Back then Arthur had been one of the few officials who provided him with straight answers on the Rendlesham case. These days Arthur was a high-level State Department spook. He continued to provide Vril with the inside information that distinguished his show from his competitors.

By providing clean information, Arthur was able to cultivate prominent sources in the media. Connections that would help at a time like this.

After Bolan convinced Vril that he indeed knew Arthur, Vril looked at his watch. "All right," Vril said. "I've got to get back to the show soon, so let's get down to it. Why are you really here?"

Bolan thought of the cover story he was supposed to lay on Vril. He and Brognola had worked out all of the details together, but the Executioner had enough leeway to play it as he saw it. That was a prerequisite for field operations like this. He had to be able to adapt to conditions.

The soldier decided to keep the cover identity but instead of manipulating Vril, he'd try to enlist him to the cause.

"I think I can trust you," Bolan said. "So I'm going to tell you the truth."

"What a refreshing idea," Vril said. "Go right ahead."

"First off I didn't come out here to do a bunch of stories on the UFO scene. They're just a cover for the one aspect of the phenomenon that I'm really after."

"And that is?"

"UFORCE."

Vril cocked his head and repeated the word. It still hadn't made it to general circulation, but he obviously knew something about it. "I've heard whispers," he said.

"What do you know about it?"

Vril shrugged. "Just rumors. Things people have told me that I haven't dared put on the air yet. These were serious people, not out to attract attention in any way. But they were extremely concerned for their safety."

"With good reason," Bolan said.

"Suppose you tell what you've got on this UFORCE."

"To start with," Bolan said. "It's a shadow operation so well hidden that much of the government isn't even aware of it. It diverted resources from genuine covert operations and agencies to create its own force. It operates from underground bases and has advanced crafts that are almost impossible to detect."

"Hold it right there," Vril said. For the first time the talk show host looked disappointed. "What you're telling me is ancient history. But don't worry. A lot of newcomers fall for that story."

"What do you mean?" Bolan asked.

"Hidden government? That's old news. Stories of the underground government have circulated since the Shaver mystery ran in *Fate* magazine back in the late '40s. This hidden government allegedly had advanced technology and the ability to influence minds."

"I don't think this has anything to do with Shaver," Bolan said.

"Don't overlook it. It matches a lot of what you're talking about. A powerful subterranean society that built a network of tunnels across the country. They were supposed to have these creatures working for them called deros, which stood for detrimental robots. They could pass for human but they could control your mind, or at the very least affect it adversely."

The Executioner shook his head. "That was pulp."

"Yes, it was," Vril agreed.

"And this is reality."

"Is it?" Vril asked.

"Yeah," Bolan said. "You're missing the point about the similarities between UFORCE and the Shaver thing. UFORCE took those myths because they were already proven. People believed in them. They embellished the myths with a few new twists so they could masquerade as this unknown force. We think it's the same force you encountered at Rendlesham."

Vril stared hard at him. "What do you know about Rendlesham?"

"As much as you do," Bolan said. "Maybe more. The ship you saw was probably a prototype, a spin-off of stealth technology applied to traditional UFO craft. UFORCE had several of those projects in development. What we don't know is how far they developed them."

"You talk about UFORCE as if it was a government project."

"It was. We know the people involved. On both sides."

"Both sides?"

"Yeah," Bolan said. "Our side and theirs. We used to work with them before they went rogue."

Vril had been around long enough to know when a deal was in the works. He'd also seen enough covert operators to realize that he was in the presence of one. This kind of intelligence didn't come without strings. "Suppose I take this at face value," Vril said. "And suppose I accept that what you're telling me is true. That means I should assume that, like our mutual friend, you are unofficially representing the United States government."

"I'd prefer to say working for, or connected to," Bolan replied.

"Thought as much," Vril said. "You know, Arthur provided me with a tremendous amount of information over the years. And not once did he ask anything in return. But now...now he sends you knocking on my door."

The Executioner nodded.

"Okay," Vril said. "But first I have one question. If what you've said is true, it's obviously highly sensitive material. So how can you say anything about it to me?"

"That's just it," Bolan replied. "I haven't even begun to talk about it. If we can work something out to our mutual benefit, then I'll tell you everything I can. You'll get the story of a lifetime when this is all over."

"And in return?" Vril asked.

"Until then, just keep on pointing me in the right direction. As a newcomer to the field, a lot of the people I have to see won't give me the same access as someone they know and trust. Someone like..."

"Like me."

"Exactly. A word or two from you will open a lot of doors. With your resources and contacts, I'll be able to gather the information I need to expose UFORCE."

"And no one will be harmed by this?"

"I can't guarantee that," Bolan said. "But that's why we're

moving against UFORCE. They've contacted hundreds of people during the past decade. Planting disinformation, staging UFO encounters. Anything to cover up their activities. They'll continue to stage events, but at the same time they might get rid of anyone in the field that knows too much about them.''

"What makes you think that?''

"They've already started,'' Bolan said.

"Then I think we've got a deal.''

Bolan told him enough about the UFORCE defection and the attacks on people who were formerly connected to it, attacks that might escalate to include UFO investigators who took too great an interest in the phenomenon.

By the time he was finished, Vril was ready to offer his help, not just as part of a deal, but part of his duty. He'd served the country once and he'd serve it again.

"You can spend the night here and we'll figure out our game plan in the morning,'' Vril said as he headed back toward his studio. "I'll show you the guest room after the show. In the meantime you can listen to the rest of the show and maybe catch up on the rest of your reading.'' He pointed at the array of esoteric reading material on the coffee table.

"Know thy enemy,'' Bolan said, picking up one of Vril's newsletters.

He was midway through the editorial when he heard Vril's voice come back on the speaker.

"This is Nicodemus Vril here, back with another hour of 'TranceFormation.' I've got a special surprise for you tonight, something that no one's heard before. Rest assured, this is truly out-of-this-world stuff.''

Bolan sucked in his breath, wondering if he'd made a mistake as he watched Vril lean into his microphone. But the Executioner couldn't imagine how a man could possibly change his tune so quickly. A patriot one minute, a turncoat the next.

"At long last I've discovered the final answer to the UFO question,'' Vril said. And then he winked at Bolan. "Up next is an interview I taped with a leading ghost hunter who thinks that UFOs are actually mental constructs, ships of the dearly departed who are trying to communicate with us. And who am I to argue?''

Vril flipped a switch on the control board to start the tape rolling, then moved closer to the mike and spoke in a near whisper.

''After you hear the interview, please call in and share your thoughts,'' Vril said. ''I'd like to know what you think about this intriguing theory about phantom UFOs. In fact, I'm dying to know.''

6

They came for the Executioner at four o'clock in the morning.

First there was the shuddering sound of rotor blades chopping through the air. Then he saw the bright beacon light of the McDonnell Douglas Nightfox as it cut like a laser through the darkness. The cone of light tracked along the center of the deserted highway twenty miles north of Black Wall.

The beacon was for Bolan's benefit, not for the helicopter crew. The lightweight chopper was outfitted with night-vision systems that allowed the pilots to run recon missions or engage in all-out combat in total darkness.

Bolan turned on the headlights of the Range Rover, briefly illuminating the ghostly volcanic terrain. He flicked them on and off twice, the agreed-upon signal. He watched the beacon grow larger as the Nightfox dropped low to the ground.

When it was about fifty yards past the Range Rover, the Nightfox hovered above the road, kicking up a windstorm of sand and debris.

Bolan got out of the Range Rover and grabbed the sniper rifle that was lying across the back seat. Then he picked up his combat vest and carryall and headed to the chopper.

As the chopper rotated to face him, Bolan saw that it was fully loaded. There was a 7.62 mm chain gun mounted on one side, and a 70 mm rocket pod on the other, designed for rapid area suppression.

The rear cabin hatch opened as soon as the struts touched down, and a man in khakis jumped onto the ground. It was the Executioner's replacement driver. Space on the Nightfox was limited and in its current combat-ready configuration there was only room for one passenger to ride along with the two-man crew.

The thrumming of the rotors made it impossible to hear, so Bolan mimicked switching a key on and off and then gestured toward the Range Rover. The keys were in it and it was ready to go.

The soldier clapped Bolan on the shoulder, gave him a thumbs-up and then headed for the Range Rover.

The white off-road vehicle had become a familiar fixture around the area these past few days while the Executioner established his cover as Gordon J. Miller, one more investigative reporter sucked into the mystery.

He'd spent a lot of time getting the lay of the land and visiting UFO witnesses, convincing them he was going to be around for a while. The last thing he wanted to do was leave the vehicle out in the open where people could come along and find it abandoned. Before he knew it, he'd be the next unsolved mystery making the rounds. UFO Researcher Vanishes In New Mexico Desert.

Another consideration was the special equipment in the modified Range Rover itself. It had been fitted out with a lot of spook gear that shouldn't fall into the wrong hands.

The driver backed up the Range Rover onto the rough terrain along the shoulder, then turned and headed in the opposite direction, back toward Brognola's command post down in the Southwest Quarry Company complex. Bolan climbed into the back of the chopper, donned a headset and then settled back into the hard seat bolted to the floor.

"Welcome aboard, Striker," the copilot said, nodding at him from the front seat. "Strap yourself in and hold on to your hat. We got to make up some time."

"The mission's been green-lighted?"

"It's being launched as we speak. Could be a hot zone by the time we arrive. Or it could still be a sneak-and-peek. Hell, you know that. That's why they sent us out here to get you."

"Right," Bolan said, subconsciously gripping the sniper rifle as the helicopter nosed into the sky. He was ready to go in quiet and take out the unsuspecting enemy if they still had the element of surprise on their side. Or he was also ready for a full-scale assault with the chopper crew.

UFORCE had been found.

At least Brognola thought so. Less than two hours ago the big Fed had located Bolan through the dashboard GPS system. Brognola dispatched the Nightflex to come out and get him even before he got Bolan on the radio and roused him from sleep to make the rendezvous.

Brognola was calling in all the special teams he could muster.

They were supposed to provide support for a COG operation that was scouring a suspected UFORCE site.

Knowing Brognola as he did, the Executioner suspected that the big Fed's units were going to vastly outnumber the Continuity of Government detachment. From the radio briefing, Bolan knew that COG was fielding a special insertion unit with high-tech masking gear that supposedly couldn't be detected by the enemy.

Supposedly.

That was the key word Brognola had used. That's why he was making damn sure there would be plenty of his own people in the area.

It was almost overkill, Bolan thought. But against an enemy like Goddard, he had to go in with everything he had.

The upper-atmosphere arsenal of satellites and recon planes that was attached to Brognola's task force had detected anomalous underground artifacts in cave formations beneath the desert. Using the same thermal-imaging technology that located underground bunkers in the Gulf War and could also make 3-D maps of subterranean archaeological sites, the recon group identified what might be an underground UFORCE installation. The thermal-imaged subterranean maps showed tunnels that seemed too symmetrical to be natural.

What almost clinched it for Brognola was the fact that the area had previously been considered by Dr. Lincoln Sturges as a suitable site for an underground government installation. It was located in the southwestern region of New Mexico in an area that jutted down like an anchor wedged between Mexican territory. The proposed site was remote enough that covert operations could be launched without too much risk of being seen.

It also had everything required for a hidden installation, including a mountain range that was suitable for tunneling and long narrow plains between the peaks that could be used as airstrips.

The tunnel expert had actually gone ahead and prepared a few different approaches for constructing an installation there. His staff at the time made some preliminary engineering drawings but the project was abandoned when an even better site was discovered.

The government might have abandoned the plans, Bolan thought. But it looked like UFORCE had gone right ahead and set up shop.

Dorian Mountain Range, Southwestern New Mexico

THE DESERT FLOOR SHUDDERED beneath the boots of the thirty-five men in sand-colored "moon suits" marching across the sparse terrain.

They slammed their feet on the ground, staggering sideways or rocking back and forth as the quake rippled across the flat and narrow plain.

It only lasted a few seconds, but every member of the search team stopped dead in his tracks. And then they waited stoically for the next tremor, knowing that it was bound to come.

Ten seconds later the earth shook once again.

This time the tremor lasted more than fifteen seconds, long enough to put the fear of God in the COG special unit. When the rocking motion subsided and they regained their balance, they looked from face to face, a picket line of spacemen spread out across a lunar surface.

The search-and-destroy operation had just become an exercise in survival.

They'd been scouring the rugged mountains and baked-earth plains for hours, checking out the canyons and caves where the satellite signals indicated there might be a possible UFORCE presence.

They were just one of several COG units wearing the multipurpose suits that blended NASA and CDC technology with the goal of making them invisible to thermal imagers and sensors.

Air-cooled coils in the outer skin of the suits were designed to reduce thermal signatures and allow the wearer to survive in a variety of harsh temperatures. Along with the advanced technology design, which included reactive camouflage, temperature controls, air tanks and biowar-resistant features, the prototype outfits were equipped with real-time computers that were keyed into overhead surveillance craft.

At any moment the COG units could use voice commands to call up a display on a small screen built into their face masks. The display could show the terrain immediately ahead of them or behind them. If they were ever unsure of their position they could summon a screen map to show them where the rest of their troops were or identify enemy locations.

Once the enemy was engaged, the displays took out all of the guesswork about their movements.

The suits were a success, but the mission wasn't. Nothing of import had happened.

Until now.

When the third tremor came, the team looked toward Major Lee Elkwood, the commander of the COG special unit.

"Hold your position," Elkwood said. "There's no sense in running until we see what we're dealing with."

Every man in the troop heard the commander at the same time and nearly every one of them had the same reaction. Instinct told them to run out of the zone. But discipline kept them rooted to their present position.

As the seconds passed, they realized it was the correct decision. Even though it was hard to stand and wait for their fate to unfold, there was no safe place in an earthquake.

The cave systems behind them were the worst place to go. And the hills across the plain were dangerously unstable. For now the best thing to do was stay out in the open and see what Mother Nature decided for them.

For the COG soldiers who were close to the center of the plain, the decision came quickly. And it was death.

Without any warning the earth groaned and opened up before them. Huge plates of rock and clay rose like mammoth tombstones. Walls of rock fell on the nearest soldiers, instantly crushing their suits and helmets and turning them into aircooled containers of blood and broken bone.

The surviving members of Elkwood's unit were split into two smaller groups, separated by the erupting shelves of rock.

A huge metallic spear crashed up through the surface, spinning wildly as it drilled through the crust. It made a tremendous whining and roaring sound and threw off a lot of heat. Then it retracted out of sight, leaving behind a gaping hole down into the earth.

Bit by bit the edges of the hole collapsed. Three men nearest the rim dropped into the dark pit, hands clawing at the air above them.

The spear crashed up through the earth again, creating another volcanic formation off to the east. It whirred and emanated a tremendous heat wave as it cut and burned its way through the earth's crust, disintegrating the sunbaked plain.

By now the COG unit knew that it wasn't an earthquake they faced. It was something much worse. It was the bulletheaded drill of a tunnel-boring machine, a locomotive-size behemoth that could rapidly cut through solid rock and leave a lining of melted glassine rock behind.

The thermal borer was a commonplace item in the construction of underground tunnels and shelters. It could bore in several directions, horizontally and vertically.

It was also an impossible weapon to defend against. In a matter of seconds it punched another hole up from the cave below. Like an ice cutter crashing up from the depths, the subterranean ram carved a jagged trail across the plain.

A long strip of desert floor caved in suddenly, instantly eroding like a bridge falling into a sinkhole. As the earth fell beneath them, a dozen more COG troops dropped into the smoke-filled abyss.

Two of the men died instantly from the fall, suffering broken necks and shattered temples from their headlong descent. Several others lay on the hard rock floor of the exposed cave system with broken bones.

The remaining COG soldiers were trampled by the man-size treads of the tunnel borer.

Moments later the sound of automatic fire erupted from the exposed cavern as black-clothed gunmen swept through the subterranean killing field. A few COG troops managed to grab their dropped weapons and return fire, but they were quickly silenced by the overwhelming odds.

From his vantage point above the trapdoor terrain, Elkwood saw two of his men cut down by the phalanx of UFORCE gunmen. He'd scrambled hand over foot on the rocky desert surface, getting there too late to keep his men alive.

But at least he could avenge them.

He propped his hands on the edge of the hole and triggered a long burst from his Heckler & Koch MP-5 submachine gun, sweeping from left to right. The arcing clothesline of lead cut down three of the UFORCE gunners before the rest of them realized they were under attack.

Bullets chopped the air over Elkwood's head, causing him to pull back, roll over several times and then come up firing from another position. He emptied his magazine, threw in a fresh clip of 9 mm rounds, and then nosed the barrel into the netherworld once again.

Around him he sensed the movement of several of his men as they approached the hellish mouth.

"Come on," Elkwood shouted to his men. "We've got them now." When he saw the massed UFORCE troops below, he felt a bit like Custer just before he charged into the village at Little Big Horn. But at least he had a temporary advantage. The underground gunners were caught in the open. They'd been too busy concentrating on mopping up the wounded to deal with Major Elkwood's counterattack.

Two COG shooters on the left side of the rim poured sustained volleys of automatic fire down into the hole. Their suppressive fire gave the rest of Elkwood's men the split-second luxury of taking careful aim at their targets.

Their precision firing took a toll, dropping several black-clad soldiers and forcing back the rest.

While his men kept up the counterattack, Elkwood called up a computer display on the lens built into his face mask.

The liquid crystal display showed that the COG force was under attack from every quarter. UFORCE rifle teams were pouring out of the caves that his men had previously scanned, catching a lot of his people out in the open.

The prototype suits had indeed camouflaged his team, Elkwood thought—camouflaged them from reality.

Maybe the low thermal signatures weren't that easy to detect, but UFORCE had obviously heard them patrolling the mountain range as they moved in and out of the caves and swept through the winding canyons and plains.

It gave Elkwood little comfort to know that they managed to uncover the UFORCE base. They'd stirred up a hornet's nest in the bargain.

The commander of the shattered COG force inched away from the rim. Now that his men were able to fight a holding action, he felt free to contact his control officer.

He tapped in the code on the handset clipped to his belt and a moment later was informing Donovan Macauley about the casualties they'd taken.

The guiding force behind COG took in the bad news and asked him for a situation report.

Elkwood gave him the most succinct appraisal possible. "Screwed and tattooed, sir," he said. "They know all of our positions and they are hitting every one of them. From the caves, from the canyons. It's like they're pouring out of an anthill."

"Cavalry's on its way," Macauley responded. "Pull back."

"That's a roger," Elkwood said, signaling his men to withdraw from the battered landscape. He looked up and saw the dark silhouette of a helicopter streaming over the mountaintops. Far behind the first chopper he saw several other small silhouettes spread out across the horizon.

BOLAN SCANNED the carnage beneath him as the Nightfox combat chopper swooped down over the mountain range.

It was almost dawn now, and in the fading darkness the Executioner could see the COG troops scattered around the plain.

A couple of them were trying to free their fallen comrades from beneath the immense slabs of rock that covered them.

The rest of the surviving members of Elkwood's immediate command were pulling back from the huge jagged trench that scarred the flat stretch of land.

The COG troopers aimed their weapons at the rim of the trench while they warily fell back. Each one of them looked left and right as if they were expecting the earth to erupt at any moment now.

On the first pass the Nightfox pilot flew parallel to the exposed tunnel while the copilot worked the FSI 2000 thermal imaging system that was mounted beneath the nose of the chopper. The cockpit display screen showed night-vision images of the underground passage and the troops milling within.

Even through the clouds of smoke and debris, the COG soldiers and the large tunneling machines showed up clearly on the green screen.

The copilot read out the menu of potential targets as they passed by and noted the position of the COG force. Elkwood's soldiers were still too close for them to let loose.

"Make another pass," the copilot said. "We can't drop the hammer until they're out of there."

The Nightfox pilot looped around and flew back down the opposite side of the trench.

As the chopper passed overhead, Bolan got another look at the men in dark clothes milling about the tunnel below. They were regrouping near the massive earth-boring machines. The fire that poured down from above had taken its toll on them.

Under other circumstances Bolan might worry about heat-seeking missiles coming up from the UFORCE position, but he'd flown on enough Nightfox missions to know that the chopper was outfitted with the FSI 2000 infrared suppression system. The "Black Hole" cloaking device prevented most shoulder-launched missiles from locking on to the chopper.

Still, his instinct kept him looking down at the UFORCE soldiers, just in case they launched something toward the fast-moving helicopter.

This time around the pilots got a better look at the huge machines that were partially covered by the tunnel outcropping.

"What the hell are they?" the pilot asked.

"Look like missiles on wheels," the copilot said.

Bolan glanced up front at the machine that was lit up on the cockpit display. There was a bright glow around the bullet-shaped nose, and at the back there was a cab full of human figures. "Tunnel borers," Bolan said. "There are at least two kinds in operation. High-speed mechanical borers and nuclear-powered cutters. My guess is that UFORCE has plenty of both."

"So what are they doing here?" the copilot said.

"Who knows?" Bolan said. "Making the base bigger? These networks never stop growing once they start. Could be a storage area, underground hangar or refueling base."

"Whatever it is," the pilot said, "let's start talking about it in the past tense. Looks like the playing field's all clear."

Now that Elkwood's men had pulled back far enough to avoid friendly fire, the Nightfox had a chance to even the score.

The combat chopper banked one more time and then made its final run at the trench.

Chain-gun fire streaked through the air and riveted the edge of the collapsed canyon. As the heavy lead chewed through the crust, Bolan could see rocks flying and earth disintegrating.

Then the 7.62 mm rounds poured down into the trench itself and ripped a heavy metal path up through the UFORCE troops. The black-clad gunners scrambled to both sides of the tunnel, tangling with each other in their hurry to get out of the firestorm.

The Nightfox chopper maintained its fire for the full length of the tunnel, then continued flying straight across the plain to make room for the other choppers that were droning down into the battle zone.

Another special-operations gunship followed the same route as the lead Nightfox and strafed the clusters of UFORCE troops just as they were recovering from the first run.

Bolan's pilot flew a complete circuit of the battlefield, taking in the firefights that were breaking out from the cave mouths and canyons on the edge of the plains. Like a colony of ants going to war, the black-clothed troops were pouring into the open.

Goddard's troops had waited until the last possible moment to reveal themselves, hoping the COG task force would pass them by. But now that they'd been found, they were making a stand.

The Executioner looked back toward Elkwood's unit and saw that several other COG troops had regrouped around their commander after the choppers made their runs. Elkwood's men were running alongside the trenches, crouching down and searching out the enemy.

"Bring me in," Bolan said.

"Where?" the pilot asked.

"Back to the tunnel. You can use the winch to drop me in."

"The zone's not clear yet."

"I didn't come down here to watch the fireworks," the Executioner said. "I'm here to make them."

"Hold on," the pilot said. "We'll all make one more run, empty what we've got and then you can go in."

"Deal," Bolan said.

The pilot radioed the other choppers roaming above the battlefield and then led the way to the huge gaping trench. As he neared the stretch of ripped-open cavern, the pilot sighted on one of the tunnel borers that was blocking the passageway and opened up with 70 mm rocket fire.

Behind him the string of gunships did the same as they neared the target, emptying their rocket pods and thumping the hell out of the machine.

Smoke and flame rose from the crevice, showing a glimpse

of the hellfire that consumed the UFORCE troops caught near the machine.

Bolan gathered up his gear as the Nightfox turned back to the tunnel. He wouldn't need the sniper rifle, not just yet. That was for measured kills, not something he wanted to count on in the middle of a firefight. He pushed the Accuracy International rifle off to the side and zipped open the canvas carryall that was sitting on the cabin floor between his feet.

The Executioner took out the P-90 and one of the side-loading 50-round clips, appreciating once more why it was becoming a standard tool for special-forces personnel who found themselves in situations like this. He locked in the clip, then retracted the stock so the weapon would be easier to hold when he descended into the pit.

Then he loaded a few extra magazines into the long side pockets of his combat vest. Along with the backup Beretta 93-R in its underarm rig, and the other munitions in his vest, he was ready for war.

The Nightfox prowled along the edge of the crevice, looking for a suitable place to drop Bolan. A good portion of the tunnel system was still dark with smoke and shadows. Through the thermal display the pilot kept watching until he saw a relatively safe area.

"Here," the copilot said, handing Bolan a pair of infrared goggles with a wire mike jutting out from the side. "Call in whatever you need. Good luck."

Bolan flipped on the goggles, slid the hatch open and then reached out for the support bar that held the Kevlar-coated winch line. He grabbed the bar to steady himself, then slipped one foot into the stirrup and hooked his arm around the drop line. Then he dug the P-90 stock into his side and aimed the barrel earthward like a metal detector in search of a hit.

"Ready," the Executioner said.

"Going down," the copilot announced, working the controls from his seat to release the winch.

As the drop line whirred into motion, Bolan could sense every vibration of the chopper as it drifted off to the left and hovered directly above the gap. He was dropping fast so neither he nor the chopper would make an easy target.

Anchored by the heavy-duty rope, Bolan descended into the smoke-filled depths of the tunnel.

When he was four feet above the floor of the tunnel, Bolan glimpsed two ghostly blurs stumbling their way through the darkness. One of them looked up and sensed rather than saw him. The other one picked up the cue from his partner and slammed himself against the wall of the cave.

The Executioner saw the barrels of their submachine guns lifting his way.

He let go of his lifeline and tumbled headfirst to the right side of the tunnel just as the short barrels spit fire.

Quick bursts of lead punched the air where he'd been hanging a moment ago. He hit the curved side of the tunnel, smashing his shoulder on a jutting rock on the way down. But he ignored the pain from the gash, as well as the jolting impact that came a second later when his knees struck the floor. Pain meant he was alive.

The momentum of his fall carried his body forward, and Bolan added a few more inches by digging in with the tips of his toes and pushing hard. He kept low to the ground as if he were diving under barbed wire.

Metal streamed overhead, slamming into the wall behind him and spraying the back of his neck with biting stone fragments.

By then Bolan was sliding on his stomach and triggering a zigzag burst of automatic fire towards the two gunners.

His return fire stitched the chest of one man with a loud sound that sent him sprawling flat on his back while his weapon spun like a top across the hard surface.

With the help of his goggles Bolan saw the phantom-like shape of the second UFORCE gunner as he recoiled from the Executioner's full-auto volley. The guy was hit in the hip and the ribs, drilling off bits of bone and tissue and flinging him against the wall.

The gunner managed to return fire and snapped off a few

short trigger pulls, but he was firing blindly and filling the cavern with whining ricochets.

The Executioner had been moving forward all the time, but the gunner's pain and panic kept him from hearing Bolan above his own screams. The soldier crouched near the opposite side of the cave, steadied himself and then zipped him with a one-second trigger pull.

The impact of the slugs knocked the hardman against the wall, coating it with blotchy bursts of red.

Bolan scanned the tunnel on both sides for any more phantom figures, then adjusted the heat sensitivity of his goggles.

The shattered cavern was a lot clearer now. He could see the bodies of the men he'd just taken out. They were no longer ghostly blurs, just ghosts.

He looked behind him and saw other heaps of bodies. Some of them were the moon-suited COG troops who'd fallen to their deaths, but most of the corpses were UFORCE gunmen who'd been chopped down by the chain guns and rocket fire.

The enemy were scattered on both sides of the tunnel, thrown there by the overwhelming firepower dispensed by the helicopter squadron. Each chopper could carry up to 4000 rounds inside the ammo box that fed the 7.62 mm man-shredders, and it looked as if most of the gunships had dropped everything they had into the cave.

At least ten enemy soldiers lay dead by the treads of a cap-sized tunneling machine that had been scorched with flame.

Bullets had pocked the surfaces of the walls and had dug huge gouges from the floor. The chain-gun fusillade had swept through the subterranean chamber like a tidal wave of lead. There was hardly a surface that was left unscathed.

Bolan looked in the other direction. At the far end, the tunnel made a sharp turn and headed into an area where the surface hadn't been ripped open. He was just about ready to head that way when he heard a clattering sound coming from somewhere above and behind him.

He whirled around, keeping the image of the tunneling machine clear in his mind so the reflex moves of his body could focus on it. He triggered the P-90 and held it down while the bullets tracked across the wall and zeroed in on the cab of the machine.

A muzzle-flash answered him from the glassed-in cab.

Once.

Twice.

Three times. The 3-round bursts punched into the floor by his feet and singed the air by Bolan's head.

The soldier kept tracking the P-90's bullet spray, hoping it didn't click empty before he reached the target.

But then an explosion of blood painted the hatch of the cab as Bolan's last burst chopped through the gunner's temple.

The Executioner fetched another 50-round stick from his vest pocket and slapped a fresh magazine into the P-90.

He walked toward the tunnel borer, keeping the barrel of the P-90 aimed at the cab just in case there was another UFORCE man playing possum. The gunner who'd almost taken him out had either been wounded or knocked out from the chopper assault. Or maybe he was just lying in wait to see who dropped in, Bolan thought. Part of a suicide squad.

The Executioner slowly prowled through the corpse-filled corridor, stopping every few steps to scan the ranks of the fallen. He'd been on battlefields before where men rose with their weapons clutched in their hands, temporarily shocked back into life. And they were reborn just long enough to squeeze off a few more rounds.

He took his time, unwilling to get taken out by a dead man. He'd been through too many wars to let down his guard.

Cold, vacant eyes looked up at him. Weapons pointed at him. But the weapons were in the cold grips of slain soldiers who'd fired their last shot. He pushed the barrels away and continued past them. They were like a flesh-and-blood memorial to the underground battle.

A memorial to treachery, Bolan thought. Just a few years ago many of these men could have been fighting side by side along with the Executioner. There were dozens of hot spots where COG and UFORCE ops had been sent into battle together. Back then UFORCE was one more weapon in the government's arsenal.

Now it was a breakaway force. The vanguard of a legion of dead men, Bolan thought, as he continued down the corridor. He couldn't rest until they were put underground for good.

The Executioner tapped the side of his night-vision goggles and flicked on the miniature transceiver that was built into the headset. Then he tugged down on the wired earpiece and inserted it into his ear.

"NF One, this is Striker," he said. "Repeat, this is Striker. Do you read?"

The tinny voice of the Nightfox copilot came back almost instantly. "This is NF One, Striker. You are on the air and we're linked to the rest of the squad. Go ahead."

Bolan updated them on his progress in the tunnel and learned that company was on the way.

Troop transport choppers had dropped off several Special Forces teams in the battle zone.

Some of the teams were securing the passes and canyons that spiraled up through the Dorian Mountain Range. They were moving down into the underground base and attempting to seal off any UFORCE escape routes.

Another team of troopers was already on the plain, moving toward the trench. "The ground team is headed by a friend of yours, Striker," the copilot said. "Sergeant Mowry. His people are hooking up with the COG unit already in place. They'll be dropping in on you any second now."

The Executioner looked at the bodies spread all around him and knew that he could use every man they could spare. The bloody mound of casualties represented just one contingent of UFORCE. There could be a lot more who were still holding up inside the base.

"The drop zone is clear. I'll be waiting for them around the bend."

He jogged down to the end of the corridor and then stopped suddenly when he was about twenty yards from the corner. From years of practice, he'd been moving silently along the tunnel wall. But he realized now there was no longer a need for stealth.

A tremendous clanking and roaring reverberated from

around the corridor. The floor of the tunnel trembled beneath his feet.

He'd seen two tunnel borers before, but only one of them had been damaged in the helicopter attack and left behind. The other machine had retreated into the depths of the underground shelter as soon as the assault began. The Executioner realized it was only a temporary retreat when he inched close to the corner and peered around the jagged bend.

Lurching down the corridor was a flame-jet tunneler with a cab large enough to fit ten men. It was the type of machine that could turn steel and rock into molten liquid.

A huge round cylinder at the front of the machine served as the platform for about forty spikelike thermal penetrators that were designed to pierce and melt their way through solid rock walls. The flame jets on the penetrators liquified the rock and then conveyed the molten material through cooling chutes that sprayed the wall with the glassine deposits.

Even if he managed to avoid being run down by the massive machine, Bolan could end up like a fly on a wall, a fly under a molten spray of glass.

With a grim fascination, the Executioner studied the advancing machine. The boring cylinder was almost as wide as the existing tunnel, leaving about six feet of clear space on every side.

Bright lights mounted above the cylinder illuminated the dark corridor with blinding candlepower, forming giant splashes of yellow on the wall.

Bolan shielded his eyes and tried to decipher the shapes that were moving alongside the huge machine as it headed straight toward him.

And then he saw them. As if the monstrous machine weren't a big enough threat, it was accompanied by a heavily armed strike team.

At least twenty men were jogging alongside the tunneler and using it for protection. Just like an infantry squad running alongside an armored tank, the UFORCE troops moved in cadence with the gigantic tunneler.

Bolan glanced long enough to take in the number of troops and the size of the machine, then pulled his head back.

He did it just in time.

The wall to his left exploded in shards as a barrage of automatic fire streamed down the corridor, almost as if the splashes of light were targets.

The first round of chattering gunfire was still echoing back and forth through the corridor when the UFORCE assault team unleashed another volley of automatic fire.

Hundreds of rounds of lead bit into the wall and chipped off huge slabs of glassy stone.

The Executioner ran back toward the first machine, knowing there was no other cover in the tunnel. A tunnel that would soon be filled with COG reinforcements.

Bolan shouted into his mike as he headed down the dark corridor and jumped over the bodies sprawled on the floor. "NF One, hold off the drop team," he said. "Repeat, hold off the drop team. We've got the mother of all machines coming our way."

The Executioner informed the chopper squadron and the Special Forces teams of his position and the position of the monstrous tunnel borer.

"Hit it with everything you've got when it comes into the open."

"No can do," the copilot responded. "You're too close, Striker. If we open up, it'll take you out, too."

"Do what you have to do," Bolan said. "There's no way I'm getting out of this tunnel unless you come in hard."

"Hold on, Striker," the copilot said. "Just hold on."

A split second later another voice came over the radio. "Striker, this is Mowry. We are near your original drop zone. Make it back there and we'll take care of you. Just lead it on, man."

"I'm telling you," Bolan shouted. "You need some heavy guns for this thing,"

"We took care of the freaking aliens, didn't we?" Mowry said. "And we'll take care of this thing. Just lead it on."

Bolan had no choice. It was coming—fast.

He continued his zigzag retreat through the bodies on the tunnel floor, hopping over the blood-slicked carcasses as fast as he could move. Just as he reached the tunnel borer where he'd nearly been ambushed before, the first sounds of gunfire echoed down the long chamber.

By then he was flat on his stomach, scrambling to safety. He clamped one hand on the large treads and then vaulted behind the tunneler, using it as a giant shield.

He caught a glimpse of the second tunnel borer just as it rounded the corner. It chewed and burned its way through walls of stone and then headed for the Executioner.

As he waited for its inevitable approach, Bolan wondered if the light at the end of the tunnel would be the last thing he ever saw.

7

The machinery of death filled the tunnel with an earsplitting whine.

It grew louder as the tunnel borer clanked and groaned toward Bolan's position.

The trapped soldier could barely hear the sound of automatic fire pouring from the troops jogging alongside the borer. But the effects were plain to see.

Gouged strips of metal fell like sleet all around him, chipped off by the blizzard of subsonic rounds that raked the side of the wrecked borer he was hiding behind.

The advancing UFORCE troops were clearing the field with fire and pinning him down at the same time. A constant stream of lead zipped through the center of the tunnel, making it impossible for him to retreat any farther.

But he wasn't going to sit and wait for them like a human sacrifice.

The Executioner nosed the barrel of the P-90 out from the metal behemoth. His angle of fire wasn't perfect, but by wedging the side-loading magazine against the upturned base of the boring machine, he increased the arc of his killzone.

Bolan triggered a sustained burst that cut into the gunners on the right side of the approaching machine.

Judging from the echoing screams, he'd taken down a few more of the enemy. That caused a temporary lull in the firing as the men on one side of the borer had to stumble over the dead and the wounded.

Bolan squeezed the trigger again, hosing the barrel in a zig-zag motion in an attempt to bank his shots off the glass wall.

As he fired the P-90, he saw the resulting pockmarks blossoming on the walls and heard the sprinkling of bullets striking the oncoming machine.

He unleashed several more volleys, sometimes bouncing the 5.7 mm rounds off the walls, other times angling them to the right side of the borer.

When he risked a glance around the edge of the machine, Bolan saw two men crumpling to the ground. Behind them there were at least a couple of bodies already down. The black-clad troops were jumping over them.

Several muzzle-flashes punched the darkness, and a fresh barrage of automatic fire singed the air around the Executioner.

Bolan ducked back behind the machine and triggered another burst from the P-90, banking them off the wall one more time.

UFORCE had the numbers but their gunners also had a lot of open distance to cover. By the time they overran the Executioner's position, their ranks would be a lot thinner.

The soldier rolled back against the wall and changed magazines with a rapid but controlled movement, then angled the P-90 again and blew off the entire clip. It bought him a few more seconds, time enough to throw a final clip into the Special Forces submachine gun.

When the 50-round magazine was gone, he'd have the Beretta.

When that was gone...

Holding the P-90 with his left hand, Bolan slipped his right hand down his combat vest and tugged a frag grenade free. He armed the grenade and flipped his hand around the bottom corner of the tunnel borer.

The grenade sailed in a well-aimed arc and dropped like an explosive egg right in front of the advancing UFORCE horde.

The flesh-shredding blast echoed through the corridor, sending another cloud of smoke and dust billowing up through the jagged roof of the tunnel.

Bolan looked skyward as the smoke cleared. A flash of movement above the ground caught his attention.

He caught a glimpse of several figures moving into position

on the upper edges of the cavern, midway between Bolan and the tunneling machine. They were crouching close to the chasm and were visible to the Executioner but hidden from the advancing UFORCE unit.

Several COG troopers were lined up on one side of the crevice with their weapons aimed downward. On the other side was Mowry and a line of men all wielding serious weapons.

Grenade launchers. Machine guns. Antitank weapons.

Mowry hadn't been kidding when he told Bolan to bring on the troops. The COG veteran had a hidden gauntlet waiting for them.

"HERE IT COMES," Sergeant Mowry said, tracking the M-203 grenade launcher across the top of the flame-jet machine as it trembled down the tunnel.

He waited until he was able to discern shapes inside the cab on top of the borer. There was room in the cab to comfortably fit about ten men in normal circumstances. But now it looked like a troop carrier. Several armed men were packed in with crew who were actually piloting the huge machine.

Mowry pulled the trigger just as the man in the front of the cab looked up. At 260 feet per second, the armor-piercing round shot out of the launch tube mounted below the M-16. The low-velocity dual-purpose grenade went through the casing and the glass, disintegrating the man's face in an explosive shower.

The men standing behind Mowry opened up at practically the same time, raining high-explosive and airburst rounds down upon the cab. The tunnel borer kept moving forward for ten more seconds before it crashed into the side of the tunnel and came to a smoking halt.

The concentrated firepower had turned the huge machine into a hearse for the men in the shattered cab. Some of them were heaped on the floor of the cab. Others were blown over the sides, leaving bloody trails marking their descents.

From the other side of the trench Elkwood's men opened up with tripod-mounted M-60 machine guns, drilling the

UFORCE troops on the ground with 100-round belts of 7.62 mm ammo.

The chattering machine guns and the airburst grenades created a firestorm that saturated the scattering force.

DOWN IN THE HAZE-FILLED tunnel Bolan stepped out from behind his cover and raked the faltering line of troops with the P-90.

Most of them were dropping to the ground from the joint onslaught, but a few turned and ran back to the opposite end of the tunnel, abandoning the boring machine.

As soon as the smoke cleared, Mowry and the other COG troopers tossed scaling ropes down into the tunnel.

Moments later they dropped down to join Bolan. Mowry was the first man to land.

Bolan nodded at the Special Forces man. "Thanks, Mowry. It was getting close there."

"Couldn't leave you down here to face all these tunnel rats yourself, could we?"

The Executioner shook his head. He'd half expected it was going to end down here in the ready-made grave. And it would have, he thought, if Mowry hadn't organized the last-minute ambush.

He was in good company.

Bolan glanced down the tunnel to where the UFORCE gunners had fled. "Let's find out where this leads," he said.

While Mowry's people followed him and Bolan down the tunnel, Elkwood stayed behind to sort out the casualties. He had some of his own men to find and, if possible, locate wounded UFORCE survivors to provide intel on the installation. It didn't look too promising. The UFORCE detachment had been shredded by machine-gun fire and grenade launchers, but there were a few semiconscious prisoners at the bottom of the heap.

After rounding the first bend and proceeding to the end of the next corridor, Bolan's group was on a slanted walkway that led back toward the mountain. They double-timed it down through the long smooth corridor and then emerged into a long and high-ceilinged amphitheater of rock.

It had been hollowed out somewhat, and several corridors had been cut from the rock, but the original natural formation of the main gallery had been made to order for setting up an underground installation. The basic platform had already been formed. On the opposite side of the cavern was a fuel dump and a lot of mechanical equipment in a garage-like square hollowed out from the rock.

"A hangar," Mowry said.

"Yeah," Bolan said. "An empty one." He glanced at one end of the mountain hangar and saw a slanted rock-lined door that was partially open. It led out to the long flat plain. The UFORCE troops obviously used it as their escape route.

Mowry shrugged. "Nothing came out of here," he said. "At least nothing that we saw."

"That's the whole idea of UFORCE," Bolan said. "Crafts that can't be detected. Silent choppers. Invisible manta-shaped ships."

"Not that invisible," Mowry said. "Remember what we saw out at Dr. Sturges's place. They can't cloak them one hundred percent. Not all the time."

"Maybe," Bolan said. "But I think you're right about this place. With all the satellites we got looking down on this mountain, they would've picked up anything that rolled out of here."

"Yeah," Mowry said. "Or the insertion teams would've bumped into it somewhere along the way. They're swarming all over the range."

The two men walked to the center of the hangar, weapons at their sides. The rest of the group did the same, taking careful aim at the mouths of the smooth-lined corridors.

Then they heard the explosions.

It sounded as if it was coming from a great distance at first. But then the sound grew louder as it echoed toward them.

"They mined the installation!" Bolan yelled.

"No shit," Mowry said.

They started running for the massive hangar door that was

levered open. Behind them came a rapid sequence of blasts. And then the tunnels themselves began to collapse.

They made it through the tilted hangar door, tumbling and sliding in the dirt just before the cavern behind them filled with fire.

Outside near the jagged trench they saw the COG task force and Brognola's special-operations units mopping up the field. Several prisoners were being marched in a single line toward one of the helicopters.

Bolan looked at the far end of the plain where three more troop transport choppers were settling down on the ground. Each one of them dropped off sticks of troopers who immediately ran through the mesquite brush that dotted the foothills, looking for any other UFORCE escapees.

The underground base, what was left it, had been captured.

Colorado Airspace

COLONEL GODDARD SAT in the central compartment of the Borealis XB-7 as it whipped through the upper atmosphere.

A combination space plane, shock-wave rider and more advanced cousin to the government's Aurora craft, the supersonic Borealis was able to cover great distances in a fraction of time required by more conventional craft.

The skin of the manta-shaped Borealis was covered with a constantly shifting digital display that reflected the sky above or below, capturing the ambient colors of any area it passed through.

With a touch of the keyboard at his fingertips, Goddard could paint the exterior of the craft with hundreds of digitally created designs. Conventional airplane running lights, cigar-shaped lights, green-and-yellow sequences, shimmering silver rods. That was the latest design to strike pay dirt in the UFO subculture. The leading researchers and lecturers were all talking about the mysterious rods seen streaking across the sky.

The rods were nothing more than computer-aided designs wedded to space-age technology. The result was a sophisticated otherworldly mask. But very few people knew how to look behind the mask of Borealis.

The ship's angular design and its adaptive temperature control reduced or altered its signature so it was practically invisible. The U.S. government had a few systems that conceivably could detect it while it was in flight, but they were still in the developmental stages.

Besides, the government didn't know what it was looking for.

The Borealis project didn't really exist. All of the prototypes that were designed and built for Goddard's covert unit had crashed or failed to perform safely on their tests. Or so it appeared on the reports he'd filed.

In reality, Goddard had successfully diverted resources from Aurora and other projects to produce the UFORCE Borealis craft, which succeeded beyond any of his dreams. As he and Captain Stevenson called it, the Borealis was a veritable "astral plane" that one moment could be seen in one location, and a short time later appear hundreds of miles away. At times, with its Mach 4 capacity, it almost seemed to move at the speed of thought.

As far as the government knew, UFORCE had only used stealth choppers and black-budget crafts like the unmanned Darkstar drones to carry out its UFORCE missions.

Goddard called up the screen display at his fingertips and watched the earth below as the Borealis soared into Arizona, heading on a roundabout way down to the base in Mexico.

The sister base in New Mexico was a shambles. The fuel depot was destroyed, and the tunnel borers were wrecked or in enemy hands. And many of his people had fallen. Good men who'd paid the ultimate price for believing in him. Goddard owed them. And he would repay them before too very long.

With so many of its assets tied up in front companies and cash-low corporations, UFORCE needed a fresh influx of funds and fuel. Both of which could be had in Mexico.

The chameleon-like craft soared through the night, heading for the border and a rendezvous with the stealth helicopters.

It was time for an alien invasion.

True, it would be a tragedy for many of the power brokers south of the border. But sometimes when the greater good was involved, such things were unavoidable.

Above all, Goddard had to keep UFORCE alive. The key to his entire operation was the Borealis that was now carrying him southward. It was a flying throne, the heart of his secret kingdom, and there was no one who could take it away from him. Especially not the COG group and its hysterical reaction to UFORCE's bid for self-preservation.

COG was mobilizing its troops and all of its political backers. That was the real danger to the country, he thought. Not UFORCE.

COG operatives were involved—no, they infested every branch of government. Yet the average American knew nothing about them.

Even though the Continuity of Government Act wasn't a secret, the purpose and power behind it was. COG had plenty of agencies at its disposal, including FEMA, the most frequent target of conspiracy-minded Americans. The Federal Emergency Management Agency was set up to respond to floods and hurricanes and riots. That was the well-known side. But many insiders believed it had a more sinister purpose, such as the creation and administration of concentration camps for American citizens who protested too strongly against government policy.

And there was also the matter of the shadow government. An entire government apparatus lay in waiting, with COG duplicates ready to step in and maintain the operation of the government. From the President down to every congressman and senator, there was a COG operative ready to step in and take control. Who could say they wouldn't make a preemptive strike and take over the government simply because they had the power to do so?

Then there were the military and covert units that COG had at its disposal. Units that were now aimed at Goddard himself. Of course it was unethical, as well as illegal, the colonel thought.

What was the sense of creating a program like UFORCE if they wouldn't use it? What was the purpose of enlisting a patriot like Goddard and not letting him lead? It defied logic, and above all, Goddard was a logical man.

UFORCE was the saving grace of the black-budget programs. The government needed a totally deniable force that could project U.S. strength wherever it was needed. In time the legitimate representatives of government would realize that. When he demonstrated that he was needed more than COG, they would take him back.

In the meantime this was the test that would prove the worth of the program once and for all. If the U.S. government couldn't prevail against them, who could?

He would demonstrate his superiority to COG, to the Justice Department, to the Special Forces, to anyone they dared to throw at him. But until Goddard was once again recognized by the government, UFORCE would have to sustain itself.

"Sir, we are entering Mexican airspace," the pilot said. "Right now we are directly above Sonora."

Goddard smiled. At times he felt as if he were riding in a private airline and the pilot was announcing the sights. But in this case the sights were actually sites. Targets for UFORCE.

"We rendezvous in approximately ten minutes."

Goddard turned his attention to the real-time map displays that changed rapidly as the Borealis continued flying south over the dry dusty plains of Sonora.

He tapped a few keys to zoom in on the target, the home base of Bastian Dominguez, one of the largest cocaine brokers in Mexico.

The former drug czar got his start in the narcotics industry by taking American funds intended to fight the war on drugs and using them to bankroll his operation. Like many other high-ranking ministers and law-enforcement figures who bought their way into power during the nineties, Dominguez helped turn the Mexican administration into a virtual crime syndicate. It sold everything from drugs to protection from prosecution.

It was a free-trade free-for-all. Even publicly owned utilities and corporations weren't safe from their corrupt overseers. After NAFTA opened up the Mexican economy, the formerly state-run businesses were sold to insiders for a pittance. In return they quickly sold the companies to foreign interests for outrageous sums. And then they kicked back fortunes to power brokers like Bastian Dominguez.

The profits of his enterprises were plain to see.

There was a private airstrip with three Cessnas lined up on the side of the runway. Several gardens and courtyards were sprinkled between three palatial buildings that made it look like a small town instead of a private residence. Luxury cars were parked in front of the main house.

Inside the desert castle there were untold riches to be had. Goddard knew as much about the drug baron's operations as the Mexican government did.

Dominguez had just completed a major distribution deal for the Sonora syndicate, flooding Texas, New Mexico and California with planeloads of cocaine. The planes returned with hard currency, which was safely locked away in a storehouse that was now under armed guard.

The money would be distributed to the syndicate partners tonight. They'd driven or flown out to the castle to pick up their share of the profits. It was a festive, not furtive occasion. Many of the guards at the Dominguez estate were officers in Mexico's antidrug agencies. Prodrug agencies, Goddard thought. There was no chance that any law-enforcement official would show his face at the Sonora soiree tonight.

According to the FBI and DEA internal documents Goddard had seen when he was still in favor, the drug payoffs to Mexican officials and army personnel were estimated to be approximately 150 million dollars a month. Just a small tithe for the cocaine billions that flooded the country.

Dominguez was smack in the middle of it.

Too bad it had to be this way, Goddard thought. He'd enjoyed working with Dominguez before and would have continued working with him if it hadn't been for his sudden losses at the desert base.

But Dominguez was his only target of opportunity. The only

other man who came close to having Dominguez's wealth was Goddard's ally in the Mexican Mafia, who also happened to be a former drug crusader. More important than money, his ally had a remote ranch that served as a UFORCE base. And he also had a belief in Goddard that was hard to come by.

He believed that Goddard had come from the stars and was on a great mission to rescue the people of earth.

That meant Dominguez was about to be removed from the earth.

Goddard increased the magnification of the display to show the positions of the guards around the Dominguez complex and then transmitted the feed to Stevenson's crew.

It was almost time for touchdown.

THE BLACK HELICOPTERS swarmed silently across Mexican airspace, unmarked and angular craft with quiet rotors and reduced infrared signatures.

Riding in the lead gunship was Stevenson, who was glad to be south of the border again. He was still smarting from the wound he'd taken in San Antonio. From now on there would always be a thin scar on his neck. But what bothered him more than the actual disfigurement was the fact that it was caused by such an insignificant man.

He'd been surprised by a shrink. A brain doctor had almost taken him out.

To make matters worse, Stevenson had to smoke the cops when they refused to leave the area and insisted that he stay until the police brass arrived. And then for the final indignity, Stevenson found himself looking into the lens of a video camera. Some reporter had caught him on film. If it had been a real war zone, Stevenson could have followed her as long as it took to run her down and take her out. But the other police cars had been closing in on them, and he was the one who had to run. Now he had people looking for her.

"We're at the LZ, Captain."

At the pilot's announcement, Stevenson pressed the shock-proof face of his watch, lighting up the time display with a greenish glow—9:02 p.m.

The guests at the Dominguez soiree were all planning to stay at least until midnight, maybe longer. Many of them would remain overnight, thinking that the armed estate was the safest place to be.

And it would be, Stevenson thought. At least for another thirty-five minutes. Then UFORCE would begin transporting some of the guests to another world.

When the chopper landed, Stevenson got out and spoke to the black-clad troops disembarking from the other choppers. They'd planned the assault hours before, and everyone knew his assignment. The feed from Goddard showed more guards than they'd expected, so Stevenson adjusted the plan accordingly, shifting the numbers of some of the strike teams.

He glanced down at his watch again—9:07 p.m. Almost time for Goddard's arrival.

Stevenson looked up at the sky and saw a black disk hovering in the sky above them, shifting into vertical-takeoff-and-landing mode. The leader of UFORCE appeared right on time.

The Borealis slowly descended, an impenetrable slice of darkness that reflected the night. It seemed like an ethereal phantasm as it drew near to the ground, gradually becoming more concrete as the ambient skin took on the color of the desert earth.

The landing struts unfolded like giant metal claws and then dug into the hard desert earth.

When the thrumming engine died out, the desert air around them suddenly seemed still and preternatural. The eerie black choppers ringed the Borealis as if it were a mother ship.

Shortly after the XB-7 touched down, the ramp lowered to the ground and Colonel Goddard stepped out. He was in a black flight suit with a side arm, ready for battle even though he wouldn't actually engage the enemy unless the operation went to hell and every gun was needed.

That rarely happened on UFORCE missions.

"Did you get the feed?" Goddard said as Stevenson approached.

The UFORCE captain nodded. "Marked their positions as soon as you transmitted. It's about what we expected from our previous intelligence gathering. We are ready to move against them, Colonel.''

"And if they change their position before we get there?"

Stevenson smiled. "Then we've got a roving team standing by to cover any change in the scenario. But I doubt they'll make any changes. These guys think they're untouchable."

"A fatal error in judgment," Goddard said, nodding. "Sometimes people are too damn confident for their own good." He looked at Stevenson's neck. The flesh-colored stitches that sewed the crusted red gash together were still visible.

"Understood, Colonel."

"Let's do it, then," Goddard said. "Bring on the aliens."

Stevenson pointed at the helicopter at the far end of the line, then gestured for the descent team to come forward.

A half-dozen men ran across the ground toward the Borealis.

Each one of them was approximately the same height and build, as if they'd all come out of a mold. The selection criteria for aliens demanded a compact form. Short, lean and muscular. They also had to have a well-cultivated sense of theatrics about them, a mandatory trait in order for them to pull off their psy-war tactics.

The men wore dull gray combat suits that enclosed them from foot to neck. On one shoulder there was a black patch embedded in the material. It was a hieroglyphic-like emblem that resembled a stylized manta ray. This was one of the legendary "alien symbols," that so many contactees and abductees mentioned in their debriefings. Symbols and indecipherable writing were a common feature in most abductions.

Invariably the witnesses also mentioned the cold and indifferent nature of the aliens who treated them as if they were specimens or curiosities. The Grays often moved around in a hivelike drifting motion as if they were being controlled by a central intelligence somewhere on the ship.

Even without their complete battle suits, Goddard's otherworldly unit looked like a frightening ensemble. Hard faced and silent, they were capable of doing whatever had to be done. They carried their "heads" in their hands as they marched across the desert sands toward the Borealis. The full-size face masks were made of a thin but extremely strong high-tech filament. Right now the masks looked like alien scalps as they flopped in the hands of the soldiers.

The alien masks had infrared lenses built into the extruding black almond eyes and radio transceivers built into the imploding ear pockets. A Velcro hem that looked like a fold of reptilian skin covered the zipper connecting the face mask to the rest of the suit.

The whole idea behind the presentation was to convince witnesses that they were in the presence of a species that was alien in most ways, but could also be distantly related to humans.

The Grays were designed as a reptilian missing link, saurian ancestors who left Earth before it was inherited by the humans.

To add to the alien effect, the face mask had a thin slit near the nose that could allow unrestricted breathing. But the mask had no trace at all of anything that resembled a mouth. The aliens had strict orders to communicate solely by radio and throat mikes so they wouldn't make any human sounding voices that could possibly give the game away.

To add to their unearthly appearance, the Grays also had gloves that gave their hands a webbed appearance. At the end of the fingers there were wolverine-sharp claws that could produce devastating wounds with one swipe.

The deceptive costuming enforced the view of the witnesses that the beings they encountered always communicated by telepathy. Although now and then, due to fallible human nature, the alien Grays occasionally emitted a few grunts and some near-human speech. It was usually a blue streak of cursing that was uttered when the Grays were surprised by panic-stricken witnesses. Despite everything that was done to the witnesses, some of them had uncontrollable instinct for fight rather than flight.

Goddard nodded his approval as the men passed by him and climbed up the ramp to the Borealis.

These were his special forces, nightmares come true to anyone who faced them. And just in case their alien visages weren't enough to shock their targets into submission, they carried an awesome assortment of so-called nonlethal weaponry with them.

The weapons could be modified depending on the need of the mission. And sometimes, even if they weren't lethal, the weapons left their victims wishing they were dead.

The alien units were a combination of the best of Hollywood and the best of DARPA. After trying out various outfits on unwitting test subjects, the UFORCE psych strike teams had settled on the Grays as presenting the most intimidating image.

In their near human form the Grays could be accepted as real beings by the majority of humans. Yet they were different enough to inspire a deep sense of unease, a sense that worlds had collided and the other world was far superior.

Goddard followed the unit into the Borealis.

Soon it would be time for Bastian Dominguez to learn about the alien menace.

8

Southwest Command Base, New Mexico

Aliens 101 was in full swing when the Executioner quietly slipped through the back entrance of the underground lecture hall. He took one of the few empty seats in the back row of the amphitheater and stretched his lean frame in the contoured chair, then settled back for the course he'd heard several times before.

Approximately seventy military and intelligence personnel were getting a briefing on UFORCE and the alien scenario. Interspersed among them were a few white-haired warriors who'd moved from clandestine jobs to high-ranking positions in the State Department.

Night school in the bunker, Bolan thought as he looked around at the men and women who'd been summoned here.

Hal Brognola's command post at the Southwest Quarry Company had gone active. Government cars and helicopters had been dropping off personnel throughout the day to go over the intelligence gathered from the captured UFORCE base. While key members of the task force hunkered down with Brognola in the second-floor war room to prepare strikes on suspected UFORCE positions, many of the newcomers were getting their first hard look at the rogue operation in the lecture hall.

The sessions had lasted through the day and drawn on into the evening as a constant procession of new groups entered into the hall for a crash course in Colonel Goddard's tactics.

The briefings had two objectives. The first and most obvious one was to educate the personnel in UFORCE ways. The second objective was to identify and separate the turncoats from the patriots.

Bolan wasn't attending this session to learn any more about the alien scenario. He was here to watch the reactions of suspected UFORCE collaborators in the audience when the lecturer sprung the trap on them.

So far they'd already isolated several collaborators from earlier sessions and brought them to the underground containment rooms, convincing them they would never emerge unless they cooperated. Although they used the threat of death on some of the more stubborn prisoners, it was ultimately an empty threat. Neither Bolan nor Brognola would ever let it happen for real. But as a psychological bargaining tool, it certainly worked wonders. They were able to cut enough deals with the prisoners to build up a lot of valuable intel about the traitors in their midst.

Some of the UFORCE collaborators were implicated in the bombing of the C-130 that crashed at Gideon. Others had played more covert roles, like setting up a chain of safehouses and rendezvous points for the rogue troopers.

And right now, four rows in front of the Executioner, was Oliver Ferguson, one of the chief architects of the safehouse network. In his current position he was a quartermaster in charge of logistics for COG special-operations teams. According to the intel Brognola's team amassed during the day, Ferguson had been secretly recruited by UFORCE years ago. Ever since then he'd helped divert assets and intelligence to the breakaway force.

Ferguson was in his midforties, a veteran of several covert operations who had performed exceptionally well in combat before opting for his behind-the-scenes position. He still had the look of a warrior about him, Bolan thought as he watched the suspect from his vantage point in the back row. The look of a warrior behind enemy lines.

Like the others who'd been summoned to the desert installation, Ferguson had no choice about responding to the call-up. To do otherwise, especially during emergency conditions like this, would be the same as admitting his guilt.

So Bolan watched and waited.

THE ALIEN THAT STARED out at the seventy men and women in the underground lecture hall was a standard-issue Gray, the classification most commonly applied to the almond-eyed, oval-skulled and vaguely reptilian beings that typically showed up during an abduction encounter.

It looked to be floating in the darkness about ten feet below the ceiling. One of its long and slender claw-fingered hands beckoned the audience in a gesture of warning or hypnotic command.

Directly below the alien stood the lecturer, Dr. Nina Krause, a woman with short cinnamon-reddish hair who wielded a laser pointer as if it were a sword. She wore a white blouse and navy-blue skirt and jacket that gave her a military look as she briefed the room full of professional soldiers. She had a pleasant and well-trained speaking voice, but conducted the lecture in a serious and almost somber style. After all, the thing on-screen was an enemy, not an alien.

From the admiring and speculative gazes she received, it was obvious that a good number of the men in the room were more interested in her than they were in the slide show. But she ignored the looks and continued her job.

With each flick of the laser beam she identified another characteristic of the Gray that glowed from the ceiling-mounted projection screen. She also spoke about the peculiar movements reported by many of the witnesses. Almost all of them said that the aliens seemed to drift or float across the floor.

Now and then she took questions from the floor, but most of the time she just rolled through her presentation. There was a lot of material to cover.

Even though he'd seen it before, the Executioner found himself drawn to the Gray's glassy black eyes, realizing that

UFORCE had chosen a potent image for their counterfeit alien force.

Click.

The Gray vanished as soon as the woman at the podium pressed the button on the side of the laser pointer.

Another alien immediately appeared on the large projection screen. This one was a Nordic, a more benign-looking alien with long blond hair and piercing blue eyes that looked out from a light-complexioned face with high cheekbones. She was also beautiful.

"The Nordics are one of the most effective disinformation agents employed by UFORCE," the lecturer said. "Their physical appeal and their exotic nature make just about anyone who encounters them feel like they are involved in something special, almost as if they've been selected to receive privileged information."

Bolan studied the on-screen image of the Nordic woman. For a moment it seemed like a goddess were glowing in the darkness. There was an ethereal, slightly dangerous quality about her.

"In much of the UFO literature the Nordics are also referred to as Blondes, for obvious reasons," the lecturer said. "Be careful if you ever meet one of them. By all accounts they are extremely hard to resist. And they, like everyone else in the UFORCE ranks, can be lethal when they want to be. If they aren't successful in recruiting or manipulating you, they just may leave you by the roadside."

One of the men in the front row raised his hand and shouted. "What about redheads? Anything we should watch out for from them?"

She waved the pointer at him and smiled. "Only if you ask them too many questions." She paused as the wave of laughter swept the room, then moved onto the abduction scenario that often accompanied UFO sightings.

"The classic abduction cases, or perhaps we should say alleged abduction cases, involve several key elements that are almost universally reported by the experiencers of these events.

Most often it is the Grays who will be seen at the actual encounters, although Blonde activity has been noted before and after. It almost seems as if they are identifying suitable targets and then following up on them afterward.''

"What about missing time?" one of the men in the front row asked, obviously someone who was versed in the subject. "Doesn't that happen in a lot of these cases?"

She nodded her head. "Spatial displacement, or as it's commonly called in the media, 'missing time,' is reported by many subjects who believe they've been abducted. This displacement can be in time, as well as location. For instance, a subject may be driving in a car and heading for a destination that is only five miles and five minutes away. But they might suddenly find themselves arriving at their destination *five hours* later than they expected. With absolutely no recollection of where they've been or how they got there. Or conversely, they could find themselves a hundred miles away from their original destination, again with no recollection of making the journey there."

As the lecturer covered some of the familiar ground Bolan heard in earlier sessions, he watched the faces of the assembled task-force operatives to see their reactions. Many of them had more than a passing knowledge about the UFO subculture, but to some of them it was obviously new and unsettling information, especially when she started to mention the latest wrinkle in the abduction scenario—the presence of military men who either directed or observed the abductions. Along with the military presence, there were also reports of silent black helicopters, cattle mutilations and a mother craft that was apparently able to change shape.

Nina Krause walked to the front of the platform and looked out over the crowd. "Now, I'm not saying that all of the reported alien abductions were done by the same group, or that the military personnel were rogue UFORCE troops. There are just too many incidents to analyze. For all we know, there could be an alien race visiting Earth and carrying out similar maneuvers. But we now have proof that many of these events were staged by UFORCE teams.''

A man from the middle row waved his hand to get her attention.

"What about the technology, then?" he asked. "How can UFORCE carry out these operations without being detected? And what if there's something behind UFORCE that we don't know about? What if it's in league with an alien force?"

A murmur of surprise spread through the crowd. These were hard-core military and intelligence people who had long been privy to inside information. They knew about the real stories behind Roswell—the test flights of experimental crafts, high-altitude parachute drops of outsized dummies, weather balloons and crash-retrieval units. But they also knew they had to consider the possibility that maybe this really was something beyond human experience.

Rather than quell the discussion and move on, Krause waited until the murmuring died down of its own accord. "Good question," she said. "If they look like aliens and act like aliens, then how do we know they aren't aliens? Rest assured that we aren't facing an extraterrestrial threat, at least in our current theater of operations. They are earthbound, earthborn enemies who happen to have out-of-this-world technology. Until now we've had little progress in locating them, but efforts are under way on the technical front to zero in on the UFORCE ships and bases. We've also made great progress in identifying UFORCE collaborators working among us, thanks to the intelligence we captured from the base south of here. In fact, it's something of a coup."

The trap was set.

Krause began talking about lists of collaborators that had been developed as a result of interrogations of captured UFORCE operatives. She also mentioned some of the locations that had been identified as possible UFORCE bases.

She then went on to talk about how several of the collaborators had actually been invited to the Southwest Quarry installation simply so they could be exposed for what they really were.

Traitors, she called them. Traitors who were currently providing leads to others in the UFORCE net.

Oliver Ferguson looked like a gnat who'd just landed on flypaper. He knew that he'd either been found out or else he was facing imminent exposure.

He looked as if wanted to bolt, but couldn't. That would give him away instantly and cut to zero his chances of escape.

Instead, as the lecturer continued her rehearsed spiel, Bolan watched as Ferguson fought to regain control. Though outwardly he looked composed and self-assured, Ferguson's body language was giving him away. He looked around the room slowly, idly, but he was really checking out the exits to see if anything stood in his way. His hands tensed up, betraying the nonchalant expression on his face that said he was just interested in Krause's revelations rather than implicated by them.

The man still felt he had a chance of getting away undetected, Bolan thought. But then Ferguson turned almost completely around in his chair, perhaps sensing the Executioner's eyes upon him.

His eyes locked on Bolan's for a couple seconds before he scanned the rest of the room and saw a few other faces looking his way.

Sergeant Mowry was in one of the middle rows, ready to cut him off if he ran toward the front of the hall. There were other men on hand to back up Mowry in case the need arose.

Ferguson nonchalantly folded up the materials he'd brought with him, a few dossiers and some other printed materials, and then stood as if he'd suddenly just remembered an important appointment he had to get to.

He walked quickly to the rear exit closest to him and hurried through the door.

By then Bolan had already slipped out the other door and was waiting for him in the hallway. He shouted out his name.

Ferguson turned, glancing behind him but not stopping. "Yes?" he said. "What is it?"

"Hold on," Bolan said. "I'd like a word with you."

Ferguson took a couple more uncertain steps before he decided to stop. But he kept looking toward the stairwell at the end of the long corridor as if he was measuring the distance he had to cover in order to break free.

"Don't try it," Bolan said as he closed in. "I'm armed. You're not."

"Is something wrong?" Ferguson asked. "There's obviously been some kind of mistake."

"No mistake," Bolan said. He stopped a few feet away from the other man, just out of striking range.

Ferguson was still in good shape and was about the same height as Bolan. Maybe a good thirty pounds heavier. None of it was fat. Even though Ferguson was no longer an active member of a special-operations field team, he still had the attitude of a dangerous man about him. He was waiting for Bolan to get within grappling distance.

The Executioner could read the man's move in his eyes. At least he thought he could. He was just short of one hundred percent certain that Ferguson was indeed a UFORCE collaborator as the other prisoners had said. But there could be no room for error. To make absolutely sure, he needed the other man to incriminate himself. The only way to do that was to put his head on the block.

"Do I know you?" Ferguson asked. He spoke softly, friendly, looking at Bolan's eyes as if he were trying to remember him.

"Probably not," Bolan said. "I'm the kind of guy people in your line of work try to avoid."

"What line of work is that?"

"Treachery," Bolan said. "Ever since you sold out to Colonel Goddard."

"Goddard?"

"Yeah," Bolan said. "The guy you've been diverting matériel to these past few years. The guy you set up the safehouse network for."

"You've been doing your homework."

"A bit," Bolan said. "But I'm not done yet. I'm supposed to conduct a full study of you."

"Well, that poses a problem," Ferguson said. "You see—"

What Bolan saw was a hand shooting toward his throat. Ferguson put all of his weight behind the move, flexing the fingertips of his left hand so they formed a killing flying wedge.

But there was nothing to kill.

Bolan sidestepped the fatal blow by a mere inch, feeling the snap of air as Ferguson's hand sailed past him. The calculated move gave Bolan the advantage for in-close fighting. The Executioner smacked the man's wrist with a palm-heel strike, clenched his grip around his forearm and tugged him forward.

Ferguson's momentum made him lurch forward a half step closer to oblivion. By the time Ferguson regained his balance, Bolan had already spun around and jammed his cocked elbow into the small of his back while still holding his arm in place.

Ferguson arched his back and stood on his toes, reeling from the full-force impact as if a lightning bolt had struck his spine. But he wasn't down yet, and Bolan wasn't taking any chances with a man who'd clearly tried to kill him.

The soldier made a split-second decision. His combat instincts called for him to back-fist the man's skull, but his strategic needs compelled him to change it at the last moment. Bolan completed the maneuver by trapping Ferguson's right arm with both hands, crouching low and flipping the UFORCE renegade over his shoulder.

There was a crack of bone as Ferguson dropped like a sack of cement onto the floor. He tried to get to his feet, then slumped against the wall and held his arm near the shoulder.

"It's broken," he said through gritted teeth.

"Yeah," Bolan said, looking down at the damaged man. "You should get that treated before you pass out."

Ferguson nodded, already reeling from the waves of nausea.

"So start talking," Bolan said. "The sooner you finish, the quicker we can get that looked at."

Ferguson rocked back and forth against the wall as the pain pulsed up and down his arm. "What do you want to know?"

"The safehouses," Bolan said. "We've got intelligence from your pals that Goddard's moving his people around to different locations, positioning them for a counterstrike. Supposedly one of them is a staging area you set up north of here. A large group is supposed to meet there."

"If you already know, then why are you asking me?"

"We have to make sure you're all telling the truth."

Bolan looked up and saw Mowry slipping through the door. The COG commando stopped a couple of inches away from Ferguson and looked down at him with a malevolent glare.

"Who's he?" Ferguson asked, jerking his head up toward the tall, lean soldier.

"Take your pick," Bolan said. "He can be an undertaker or an orderly. All depends on whether or not you talk."

Ferguson talked.

DR. NINA KRAUSE SCANNED a thick metal binder full of raw data from Colorado and New Mexico abduction cases that had been collected for her in a second-floor office of the Southwest Quarry installation. She was reviewing them in hopes of discerning a pattern, using the times and locations to figure out likely bases where UFORCE might be operating from.

Her last lecture of the day was over, but her work had just begun. Like everyone else at the facility, she would probably work through the night. They had to pursue UFORCE while the trail was fresh.

As she worked her way through the reams of material, she listened to a classical CD in the laptop computer she always carried with her. It filled the room with the short baroque bursts of harpsichord, violins and cello from the *Bizzarie Universali,* William Corbett's collection of concertos.

It was the perfect antidote to the soul-numbing and mind-bending work she'd been doing for Hal Brognola and his operatives. Research and intelligence analysis was one thing. Taking part in an actual operation against collaborators was another. The uplifting and dreamlike pieces helped take her mind off the war she was helping to fight.

But a few minutes later a six-foot-tall reminder walked into her office after knocking on the door.

It was the man known as Striker, and he was definitely someone highly regarded by the people running the show.

The man with the weathered face and ice-blue eyes had been given carte blanche here at the facility. Even though he walked around in khaki fatigues like many of the other rank-and-file soldiers, there was no doubt he was a different type of soldier.

He was a man used to command. Whatever he wanted he got. And right now he wanted her to move on to the next phase of the operation.

"You did great work out there," the lean soldier said as he pulled up a hard metal chair and set it right beside her desk chair so they were literally seeing eye to eye. He was always like that, she thought. Every contact she had with him so far was up close and direct. A straight-shooting kind of guy. "Those presentations helped us flush out some of the key UFORCE operatives."

Krause shrugged. "Maybe they did," she said. "But I've got to admit it's difficult for me to be a part of this."

"It would be a hell of a lot more difficult without you," the soldier said. "We needed someone who knew the UFO field inside out. Someone who also knew how to present the info and bait the hook."

"I just worked in the material you provided," she said. "To tell you the truth, I wasn't sure how it would turn out. Until now I was only involved in the academic side of things. Strictly hypothetical. Never thought I'd work on an actual operation."

"First time for everybody," Striker said. "You heard the call and you answered it. And for that I want to thank you."

She smiled. "That's nice to hear," she said. "But I've got the feeling you didn't come up here just to tell me that. There's something else, isn't there?"

"Yeah," he said.

"What now?"

"Remember when we spoke before about the possibility of feeding some disinformation to the other side?"

"Of course," she said. "Back then you and Hal said that it was only a possibility. The main thing was finding the collaborators."

"Right. We've rounded up the ones we wanted most, the men who posed the greatest danger to us or who could provide the best intel."

"What about the others?" she asked. "You're not going to let them go free, are you?"

The soldier shook his head. "No, not really," he said. "But to them it's going to look that way. We're going to cut some of them loose and place them under surveillance to see where they can lead us. Satellites, AWACs, ground-based observer teams. The works. They won't get away from us."

"You said some of them, Striker. What about the others?"

"They're waiting downstairs."

"What?" She had an image of another room full of people waiting for the dog and pony show she'd already performed more times than she cared to. "I thought we were through with the briefings for the day."

"This is different," he said. "We've gathered this last group in one of the conference rooms down below so they can get one last briefing from you and a COG commander. Remember, these are all suspected collaborators who've already seen your sanitized lecture, the one where you made no mention of the operation to identify UFORCE collaborators. They regard you as one of our top experts."

"That's a plus," Krause said. "Considering that only seven days ago I didn't know word one about UFORCE."

"Yeah," the soldier said. "But they don't know that. As long as they think you're in the loop, we can use you to feed some disinformation to them."

"Such as?"

"Such as convincing them they've been assigned to a special operation," he said.

"And this special operation is a bogus one?" she ventured.

"Right," he answered. "We want to plant some false information with UFORCE. It's connected to the San Antonio killings. Did you have a chance to get familiar with the materials?"

She nodded, remembering the details of the exhaustive briefing she received on the murders of Dr. Schyler and the San Antonio police unit that showed up while UFORCE was still on the site.

"Run it by me."

"Mind telling me why?"

"Not at all," he said. "Before we send you in to convince them, I want you to convince me that you know all the details."

"Why you and not Hal?" she asked. "He led the briefing I saw on the San Antonio aspect."

"Because this particular operation is something I came up with and that makes it my responsibility," he said. "Because of me people's lives will be at stake and I'm not going to take any unnecessary risks."

"Just the necessary ones," she said.

The soldier nodded.

"Okay," she said. "If that's what you need."

"It is," he said. "Let's hear it."

She recounted all of the information she'd absorbed about the San Antonio case, beginning with the hit at the professional building and the homicide squad's subsequent visit to Schyler's house. When the detectives interviewed his wife, they found out about his connection to UFORCE and a duplicate set of notebooks he kept that detailed his earlier work for Colonel Goddard. She'd had a chance to view photocopies of the notebooks. As soon as they realized what they had in their hands, the detectives passed the information up through channels, which was then brought to the attention of Hal Brognola.

Schyler's wife was moved to a new location and provided with around-the-clock protection from the Justice Department.

Then there was the matter of the videotape. Apparently a couple of stringers who were listening to their scanners arrived at the scene just in time to film the execution of the police officers. The woman who actually took the film was chased by the leader of the hit team, which understandably made her a bit apprehensive about announcing what she'd captured on tape.

Instead of going to the television networks and risking exposure—knowing that they'd make her a part of the story and a target for the killers—she made a few approaches to law-enforcement agencies. Since the tall man she caught on videotape appeared to be some kind of spook, she contacted the FBI instead of the CIA. Again, that brought her into the realm of Hal Brognola.

Krause added a few more details from the briefing, then said, "And here we are now." She looked at the man who'd listened impassively as she spoke, not giving a clue about what he thought of her version of the facts. "Well?" she asked. "Do I pass?"

"With flying colors."

"Now what?"

"Now that you know the real details, we'll add a few false ones to lead them where we want them."

"What do you want me to do?"

The soldier paused for a moment. "I want you to make them think they're part of an effort to track down the stringers who are peddling the videotape. And Dr. Schyler's incriminating notebooks."

"How?"

"To start with, make them think that the stringers have been trying to sell the tape of Schyler's murder to the highest bidder, and that another group is making the rounds with pirated copies of the notebooks. And make it sound as if these notebooks have a lot of details about UFORCE operations, locations and personnel."

"I can do that," she said. "But who are they supposed to be selling them to?"

"Nicodemus Vril, for one."

"The radio guy?"

"Right. The one with the syndicated show."

"But that'll make him a target," she said.

"Yeah," he said. "That's the idea."

"Who else are they supposed to be dealing with?"

"There's a cable TV production company in Colorado called Ground Force Productions," the soldier said. "They make a lot of documentaries on military subjects and they also do a series about unexplained mysteries and unsolved crimes. Make it seem like they've been approached to buy both the tapes and the notebooks."

"Ground Force Productions," she repeated. "Is this a real company?"

"As real as it has to be. They've got warm bodies, a production studio and a lot of programs on the air."

"Some kind of independent company?"

"Sort of," he said. "They're sponsored by a rich uncle."

"Uncle Sam?" she said.

The soldier nodded. "The same."

"So," she said. "In this version of the story, does either the production company or the radio show have the tapes?"

"Not yet," he said. "Tell them the sellers are trying to negotiate a higher price."

"Understood," Krause said. "I see where you're going with this, but won't that put a lot of people in harm's way? Like Vril. And the people at the production company?"

"It's going to be dangerous for everybody if we go ahead with this," the soldier said. "But it'll be more dangerous if we don't."

He outlined the plan for her, giving her just enough details about the alleged stringers and their possible whereabouts to bait the trap for the UFORCE special-operations unit.

When he was finished, he leaned closer and said, "I know this is hard. But I know you can do it when you get down there in the briefing room."

"What about you?" she asked. "Will you be down there with us?"

"No," he said. "I'm going out in the field. Following up on some of the intelligence."

"Don't follow too close," she said, aware that the field he was going into was a killing field. "I'd like to see you get back here."

"I'll do my best," he said.

LESS THAN ONE HOUR later Mack Bolan was sitting in a dark room in the middle of an abandoned roadside saloon, waiting for the rendezvous of UFORCE operatives scheduled to arrive in the desolate ghost town of Ark Springs.

It was as dusty and dry as the baked riverbed that ran beside it, a town that hadn't seen water for nearly a hundred years. Back in the fifties it was temporarily resurrected by a private owner who restored the original buildings and added an Old West hotel, hoping to make it a tourist attraction for people passing through western New Mexico.

But the hotel dream died out just as the original town had, and soon all of the buildings passed into the hands of the state. Then it passed into the hands of time and the desert.

Now it was in the hands of the Executioner.

Just as Ferguson had said, the saloon had become a weapons cache, a temporary way station for UFORCE troops on the move. Bolan had seen the crates of weapons that Ferguson's crews had secreted in the sunken room below the bar. He'd left everything untouched.

Sergeant Mowry had done the same thing in the building next door, an old newspaper that still bore the name The Ark Springs Free Press on a handwritten sign above the shattered window front.

There were a few other COG commandos hidden in some of the other buildings, but the main force was miles away. They didn't want to give anything away to the UFORCE groups descending on the area.

Ark Springs was the key staging area in this section of New Mexico. There were several other launching pads that Ferguson set up throughout the state, but this was the closest to the

Southwest Quarry Company. As soon as the UFORCE collaborators received their summons to the installation, they'd passed the word on to Goddard.

When the briefings were over, the UFORCE teams planned on hitting Brognola's base of operations.

The Executioner meant to change those plans.

Though he'd left the weapons cache alone, the soldier had plenty of his own armament spread out through the saloon. He was ready for room-to-room or house-to-house fighting.

The fighting would begin any moment now, he realized, when he heard the pitched whine of desert bikes echoing in the distance.

He followed the progress of the bikes by the sound that grew louder and louder as they bounced over the hilly desert terrain on the outskirts of town.

And then they were on the rutted and eroded street outside, kicking up trails of dust behind them. The whining engines dropped down to a throaty and sputtering growl as they cased the town.

Bolan peered through a crack in the boarded windows of the saloon. He saw six of them. They were in black from head to toe, helmet, jackets and boots. The bikes were painted a dark shade of black, and there wasn't an inch of chrome anywhere on them. Even though the headlights were off, they were shielded with black rubber housings. This was definitely a group of night riders who didn't want to be seen.

The six riders rode in a small circuit that covered both sides of the street, looking down the alleys, peering toward the buildings.

Maybe there were a few more down the street. The Executioner couldn't tell from his observation point, but it sounded as if there were at least a couple of desert bikes prowling at the far side of town.

However many riders there were, he thought, it was hardly enough to be a strike force. Obviously just an advance team checking out whether or not their rendezvous had been breached.

The Executioner watched for a few more seconds, long enough to see three of them heading his way and lining their bikes up so they faced the saloon. He slowly pulled his head back from the window. He didn't want the intensity of his gaze to alert them. These were veteran troopers who might sense his presence rather than see it.

The engines died suddenly, switched off in unison.

Then there was a long silence as the three men sat on their bikes waiting and listening, looking over the facade of the saloon.

After several more seconds Bolan heard a curt voice directing his men to move forward.

From farther down the street he heard another man giving out similar directions. That meant there were at least two of the three-man teams in the immediate zone.

Three riders for Mowry. Three riders for the Executioner.

Footsteps kicked through the dusty street, then rumbled up the steps onto the boardwalk, heading to the rickety wooden doors of the saloon.

Bolan lifted the sound-suppressed Beretta and leaned close to the wall.

He'd chosen a table closest to the front of the building in a small alcove that was hard to see from the center of the saloon. He figured the location would give him a window of opportunity for about thirty seconds before they realized someone else was in the saloon.

Then it was going to be a showdown.

Heavy footsteps paused at the entrance. Then the doors creaked open and poured in a slice of moonlight. Three long shadows were painted on the floor. Two of the shadows seemed to be holding disembodied heads in their hands as their helmets swayed from their straps.

One of the riders flicked on a flashlight and aimed it at the back of the long narrow dance hall. The beam passed through a swirling cloud of dust motes stirred up by the three gunmen.

The light flickered across the cracked mirror behind the bar, then darted over to the corner where Bolan was hiding. The cone of light passed just a few inches away from the edge of the wall Bolan was pressed against. He stayed perfectly still, barely breathing as the beam searched the wall across from him inch by inch. For a moment he wondered if he'd miscalculated and somehow given his presence away, half expecting a volley of bullets to follow the light and cut through the wall.

Then the beam of light moved on.

"Looks clear," the man with the flashlight said, stepping into the center of the saloon where Bolan could get a good look at him without showing himself. He was holding the long-barreled flashlight in one hand and a heavy revolver in the other. The barrel of the revolver followed the light. Just like a two-gun kid, Bolan thought. The man was really getting into his surroundings.

The other two men followed closely behind. They were a lot more relaxed now, figuring the slow scan of the building would have turned up any intruders. They dropped their helmets on the table

Bolan raised his arm slightly, trigger finger pointing at the man with the flashlight. The Beretta's selector was set on 3-round-burst mode. He had a full magazine and he had surprise on his side.

He needed them both if he was going to take one of these UFORCE riders alive. It was a dangerous game he was about to play. Each UFORCE captive led the way to the next. If he just wasted them all, it would be that much harder to climb up the next rung of the ladder.

"You stay here," the leader of the crew said, "while I check out the weapons."

One of the men grabbed a chair and dragged it across the floor, then sat at a table. The other man stood beside him. Both held their weapons at the ready.

Not good, Bolan thought. As long as they were grouped together, he had a chance to keep all of them in the line of fire. But if he gave them a chance to spread out, the odds changed dramatically. There would be too many angles for the geometry of death to be on his side.

"Don't move!" Bolan shouted. "Not the flashlight. Not the guns."

All three men froze for a split second. Then the flashlight moved toward Bolan's position.

Bolan zipped him with a 3-round burst that knocked the flashlight from his hand and turned off his lights forever. The gunner got off one last trigger pull and blasted a hole in the ceiling on his way down to the floor.

As the loud echo from the revolver filled the room, Bolan dived to his left and fired a second burst from the Beretta. The trio of 9 mm rounds took out the UFORCE gunner sitting at the table. They hit him chest high just as he opened up with his submachine gun. His unsilenced rounds chewed into the alcove where Bolan had fired from a moment ago.

The gunner was still trying to correct his mistake and track Bolan with the barrel of his weapon when the life drained out of him. His dead hand fell on the table, and the weapon clattered to the floor.

The third man had stepped back from the table, watching for the flashes from the Executioner's weapon. He opened up with a full-auto burst that ripped through the tables and chairs near the bar, kicking up a shower of splinters.

By then Bolan was at the far end of the bar, still scrambling across the floor. He swept the barrel of the Beretta to his right and blew off six more rounds at foot level. The 9 mm slugs cut the man's legs out from under him, and he went down face first on the floor.

He was alive and bleeding heavily, and though he could barely move, his hand snaked across the floor toward his dropped weapon. Bolan kept him covered with the Beretta as he hurried forward and kicked the submachine gun out of his reach.

The UFORCE commando cursed at him between gritted teeth.

"I told you not to move before," Bolan said. "That warning's still in effect."

After making sure the man wasn't an immediate threat, Bo-

Ian hurried over to the window and looked out at the street. There was nothing there but the three empty bikes in front of the saloon. No UFORCE riders were coming his way.

He heard gunfire coming from the building next door. First there were several loud bursts of automatic fire that were immediately followed by Mowry's suppressed return fire. Several more shots echoed from farther down the street. The shooting was over quickly, the way most one-sided gun battles were.

No matter how well-trained the soldier, there was little he do against another professional who was just waiting for him to walk into his killzone. Especially when the ambusher knew every inch of the room and where he was most likely to run.

Bolan stepped out through the door and called down the street. Mowry's reply came immediately. Three dead. He was clear. Beyond him two more COG commandos called out their situation report. Two dead. No prisoners.

The Executioner headed back inside to the wounded man. He was lying flat out. Blood saturated the floor near his right ankle and spread out in a thick crimson puddle.

Bolan grabbed the back of his shirt, twisted it for leverage, and then tugged him into a sitting position. The man was heavily built, and just about all of it was muscle. Bolan felt him tensing up as if he were going to try something even in his wounded condition.

He released his grip.

The man dropped to the floor, flattening his palms to break the fall. His reflexes were good. "What the hell'd you do that for?" he shouted. He turned on his side, face twisted in pain from the bullet-shattered bone. He was gasping hard, fighting off the effects of shock. But he also looked as if he was acting.

"Your wound's bad," Bolan said, remembering all the times he'd seen apparently dead men take out someone who let down their guard. "Not as bad as your friends over there." He gestured with the Beretta toward the fallen UFORCE commandos, then brought the barrel back to the wounded man. "Sit tight and you won't have to join them."

"I need help," the outlaw soldier said.

"Convince us you're worth saving and we'll take care of you."

"Us? There's more of you?"

"Yeah," Bolan said. "More than enough."

A moment later Mowry and the two other COG troops filed into the bullet-riddled saloon. The two khaki-clad men looked around the room, then went back to the doorway to stand guard.

Mowry strolled over and looked down at the wounded man, then glanced at Bolan. "Is he talking?"

"Not yet," Bolan said. "He wants a nurse."

Mowry laughed. "Screw that," he said. "Let's just plant him in Boot Hill out there and be done with it. Not much he can tell us except there's a shitload of dirty mercs heading our way. All we have do is call in the choppers and smoke every last one of them."

Bolan looked down and saw the calculations going through the rogue trooper's eyes. The prisoner looked up at Mowry and saw someone who looked capable of taking him out without a second's thought.

"It's up to you," Bolan said. "I already asked him nicely. Try it your way."

"Wait!" the man said. "I can give you the details of how they're coming. They've got a convoy of freight trucks..."

Mowry feigned surprise that there was any worthwhile intelligence to be gained. "You're halfway there, bud," he said. "Keep it coming and you just may walk again."

The UFORCE commando gave up everything he had. Three truckloads of renegade shock troops were barreling across the state highway in specially outfitted trucks. As soon as they received the all-clear signal on their satellite radio—two clicks, a three-second pause and two more clicks—the convoy would detour south to Ark Springs.

Bolan radioed the intel to the commander of the Nightfox squadron assigned to the ghost-town operation.

"Roger that, Striker," the commander said. "We're getting them on our screens. Don't worry about them getting to your position. Our ground team is setting up a midnight inspection station as we speak.''

THE MIDNIGHT INSPECTION station was a blockade of two police cars parked nose to nose on a two-lane road about eight miles north of Ark Springs. As soon as the headlights of the first truck rounded the turn a half mile away, the drivers of both cars turned on the flashing lights. They bolted from the cars and ran up the nearby ridge to join the COG rifle team lying in wait.

There was little doubt the trucks would reveal themselves by running the blockade, but they had to make sure the prisoner's intelligence was legit. For all anyone knew, until the trucks actually made a break for it, they could have been a convoy being led in the wrong direction.

But the driver of the first truck sped up as soon as he saw the barricade. By the time it smashed through the patrol cars, it was going at least seventy miles per hour. The metal-reinforced ramming grille speared through both cars and sent them spinning off the road with their headlights aiming into the sky.

The second and third truck followed suit, racing past the smashed patrol cars and on toward the ghost-town staging area.

One mile south of the blockade the drivers noticed dark blunt-nosed shapes streaming across the sky on both sides of them.

The night was filled with helicopters.

The pilots were flying lights out and low to the ground, using infrared night-vision systems to track the convoy.

The lead chopper flashed its beacon on the windshield of the first truck, totally blinding the driver. Instead of stopping, the driver toughed it out and zigzagged down the center of the road. Several barrel-flashes lit up the passenger side of the truck cab as the UFORCE shotgunner tried to rake the Night-fox with automatic fire.

That was the only weapon fired by the entire convoy.

One second later a rocket crashed through the passenger-side window and obliterated the gunner in a flash of smoke and fire. A chain gun raked the full length of the truck.

Another chopper fired two rockets into the road just ahead of the truck engine, blasting the ground out from under it.

The heavy wheels jumped off the ground, and the entire truck tipped over. It rolled sideways down the road for about thirty yards before it tumbled off into the desert.

By now the two other trucks saw what they were facing. Death from above. The second truck hit the brakes and screeched to a stop just yards away from the rocket-blasted gap in the road.

The third truck stopped right behind it.

As a half-dozen blinding lights splashed across the windshields of the trucks, the drivers quickly jumped down onto the road with their hands over their heads.

While the Nightfox choppers kept the rogue troopers in the spotlight, COG units rushed forward from both sides of the road and began leading the UFORCE soldiers from the truck one by one.

There were no casualties in either of the trucks that stopped, but most of the men in the first truck were killed in the rocket assault or in the crash, and even now were moving on to a ghost town of their own.

9

Sonora, Mexico

"There's something out there," Estefan Ruiz said, alerting the other guard who was protecting the southern perimeter of the Bastian Dominguez ranch. He'd been on similar duty several times before, but this night he might actually be earning his keep.

Ruiz slung the strap of the submachine gun down his arm and gripped the cold metal weapon. He aimed the barrel out at the darkness.

Nothing.

He swept the barrel from left to right, tracking across the brush-filled horizon and the rolling dunes.

After a half minute of silence he heard the other guard's familiar harsh laugh. "It's only the wind," Teodoro said. "Or maybe it's the white powder. You sample too much of that stuff for your own good, Estefan. It makes you jumpy. Makes you see things. Like these ghosts you're talking about."

"Must be good stuff," Ruiz said, glancing at the other man's weapon, which was also pointed at the ghosts he'd imagined, "if it can make you see them, too."

"I'm just humoring you, my friend," Teodoro said. "That's all."

"Then I commend your performance," Estefan responded. "You're very convincing."

Teodoro shrugged. Even though he had indeed mocked his fellow guard, he'd felt the same sudden uncertainty as Ruiz.

Fear was contagious in the dark of the night. But sometimes it was the proper emotion. Like now. Something was out there! Something was moving in the shadows.

For the first time in years Teodoro felt adrenaline coursing through his system and waking up the instincts that had lain dormant for so long. There was a thundering in his chest, and he could hear the blood pounding through him.

But then the alarm died as quickly as it flared. His pulse gradually slowed and returned to normal. There wasn't anything dangerous out there after all, he realized. It was just a trick of light. Clouds were moving overhead, now and then permitting the moon to shine down upon the cluster of brush. The branches were indeed moving, but it was due to a spectral desert breeze. Exactly as he'd told Ruiz.

Teodoro was almost disappointed. He'd almost been a soldier again. But just in case, as his eyes drifted across the horizon he kept his submachine level, ready to puncture the shadows with automatic fire. In his hands the weapon looked almost like a toy. The back of his hand was too large to fit inside the carrying handle. That kind of thing always bothered him, making him think that one of these days he would adopt a strict regimen and get back in shape.

Teodoro thought back fondly on the days when he was a fit and fighting man. Right now his military uniform looked like a badly chosen costume that was too taut around his mountainous stomach and broad, soft shoulders. His physique had started to balloon into its present gluttonous state soon after he was forced to abandon the principles that caused him to enlist into the army.

He had truly been a soldier once. Though he'd never actually done any fighting, he was always prepared to do so. But it wasn't meant to be. These days the only military skill he required was the ability to look the other way. He'd been a courier, a guard who protected drug shipments, watched airstrips, took his cut and went home.

It wasn't his fault.

To survive in the military, the police or the interior ministry, he had to go along. He had to take the payoffs. If he refused, he would've been quickly put out to pasture. Or suffered an even worse fate. The ranks of the dead were filled with the names of noble soldiers and police officers who had actually tried to stop the cocaine trade. They were killed by their own superiors, a lesson that stayed with Teodoro whenever he thought of getting out.

So now he stood guard for one of the most corrupt and respected men in all of Mexico, Bastian Dominguez.

Both guards stood there with their short-barreled Colt Commando submachine guns nosing across the dark desert. The close-quarter weapons had been part of a shipment of surplus arms the U.S. Army provided to the Mexican government to help them in their antidrug campaigns against rebels and cartel kingpins. Those were the real phantoms, Teodoro thought. The kingpins who were supposedly caught by Mexican police. He shook his head. None of them spent any time in a real jail. And if one of them was allegedly killed in a shootout with the police, it was always some patsy's dead body that was found. All part of the great charade.

A charade just like this guard duty. No one would dare come for them.

After the brief moment of alertness subsided, Teodoro lowered his weapon. "Do you still see anything out there?" Teodoro asked.

"No," Ruiz answered. "It's just as you said. The wind is our only enemy this night." He laughed and he, too, lowered his weapon.

The two men relaxed against the exterior courtyard wall, lighting up smokes to kill time.

After the cigarette break they resumed their meandering patrol along the stone wall, idly cradling the submachine guns in their arms with the flash suppressors pointed toward the night-shadowed hills.

THE WAR-PAINTED FACES of Captain Stevenson's men stayed low to the ground as they advanced toward the south wall. The green-and-brown streaks of camouflage that ran from their temples down to their necks matched the shadowy terrain they moved across.

They inched steadily forward, black shapes who saw two dead men standing guard. By now it was all over for them. Their actual deaths were just a formality.

Crosshairs were lined up on each guard's head at all times in case they noticed the impending attack. As one half of Stevenson's people moved forward, the other half zeroed in on them. They continued in that manner until they were at the edge of the brush, lying prone on an incline that looked up at the estate.

Stevenson glanced at the man with the crossbow who was lying on the ground two feet away from him.

Chet Matthews had been Stevenson's backup for almost two years now, a considerable accomplishment in light of the number of missions he'd had to go on. The UFORCE warrior managed to stay alive mainly because he followed orders without question.

Right now Matthews was sighting the Special Forces crossbow on the larger of the two guards, the gigantic man on the right. The crossbow was fitted with a telescopic sight and was designed for long-range quiet kills. To prevent detection, it was painted with a dull black matte finish. The spear-head bolts were exactly the same color.

Stevenson looked to his left and saw that the other man was also zeroed in on his target. Each man had his crossbow cocked, a bolt in place and a finger on the trigger. "Take them," he whispered.

TEODORO THOUGHT it was a bat at first when he heard the strange fluttering sound cutting through the air.

Then he heard a loud *thock* coming from several yards to his right. He turned his head just as Ruiz made an awkward leap in the air. It would have been comical if not for the tortured expression that flashed upon his friend's face.

Ruiz's feet were practically lifted off the ground as if he

were a marionette dancing on invisible strings. At the same time as his feet left the ground, his head was jerked violently toward the wall.

A black bolt sprouted from the side of Ruiz's temple. Spouts of blood erupted from the shaft and ran down the side of his head, blossoming around his awkwardly twisted throat. His body sagged abruptly, as if all of the air was let out of him and he slumped against the wall.

By the time Teodoro realized what happened to his friend, he had a fleeting awareness that the same thing was about to happen to him. It was too late to do anything but pray to God for a miracle. But Teodoro had given up all rights to miracles when he'd joined this unholy cause.

He snapped his head back toward the brush just as a steel bolt ripped through the front of his skull. He'd heard that strange thrumming sound again, a sound that seemed to explode inside of his brain and drown out the clamoring thoughts trying to emerge all at once.

The bolt knocked him off his feet and speared him to the wall.

Sheets of blood cascaded down over his eyes, painting his last look at the desert a dark and deep red. With his last conscious thought, Teodoro admonished himself for not paying more attention to his instincts. He knew now that some unknown enemy really had been lurking out in the desert all along.

And the breeze that he'd heard sifting through the branches was the whisper of death telling him it was coming. It was a sound he had refused to hear.

STEVENSON'S TEAM RAN forward, glanced quickly at the sentries to make sure they were silent forever, then threw rubber-coated grappling hooks over the courtyard wall.

They tugged hard on the fastened ropes to lodge the tines in place, then scaled the walls in a matter of seconds, walking halfway up until they could sling their arms over the edge and then scramble up the rest of the way.

Stevenson peered down into the courtyard and quickly scoped out the guards. There were about ten of them walking without the faintest idea that security had been breached.

Glorified chauffeurs with guns, Stevenson thought. They were clearly enjoying themselves, listening to the live festive music that drifted across the courtyard from the main house. Soft guitars and horns and plaintive voices romanticizing a Mexico from a hundred years ago.

The guards were so inexperienced in the ways of real combat that they'd actually expected any assault to come through the front gate. For that reason another handful of them gathered just inside the gate, weighted down with holstered firearms and the belief that they could face anything that came their way. But to do that, they had to see it coming.

Stevenson looked across the courtyard, watching the other teams silently appear on top of the walls. The same maneuvers that his team just performed were simultaneously carried out from every direction.

Sentries silenced.

Walls breached.

Remaining targets acquired.

Stevenson could make out the other assault teams with his naked eye, but he had to make sure that each of the team leaders could see him. He raised his night-vision scope and scanned the opposing battlements where they waited with their UFORCE troops. Just as he expected, he saw the infrared images of his team leaders looking back at him through their night goggles.

He raised his hand and pointed to each team leader in succession, waiting for a return signal before moving on to the next man.

They were all locked on to him, waiting for him to trigger the assault.

Stevenson's men had already zeroed in on their assigned targets by the gates. If any one of the guards happened to look up, Stevenson's people could take them out at once. But in order to achieve the full UFORCE effect, they had to wait for the arrival of the ultimate weapon.

It appeared one minute later when the Borealis skimmed across the skies and moved through the wispy clouds above Sonora.

Goddard had been watching the progression of the assault from the moment it began. Now he was ready to join the party.

As the Borealis drifted slowly toward the Bastian Dominguez fortress, Stevenson chopped his hand down. The soft staccato chatter of sound-suppressed Heckler & Koch submachine guns rumbled from the upper walls.

The guards by the gate fell instantly, riddled with bullets from temple to torso. They toppled over each other and landed in a tangled, bloody heap. Most of them still had their weapons in their holster. Two guards actually managed to snap open their holsters and grab metal, but it was a useless gesture. A brace of automatic fire drilled through their wrists and hands and practically severed the grasped weapons from their arms.

Two teams had been tasked to the gate unit, although one would have sufficed. The men were dead at least twice over. UFORCE was practiced in the art of silent slaughter and had used the same teams to carry out similar assaults.

The other teams on the courtyard walls had been tasked with handling the remaining guards. They opened up with a withering cross fire that rained down upon the unaware soldiers. A clothesline of lead swept them off their feet

The perfectly aimed shots came all at once, almost as if they'd been fired from one single weapon.

Strains of music accompanied the short death throes of the men in the courtyard who dropped to the ground quickly. Some of the guards looked upward, eyes wildly searching for their exterminators. But all they saw were bright flashes of fire streaming down at them from the darkness.

The automatic fire ceased as soon as the guards stopped moving. A deathly stillness settled over the courtyard. It had just become a cemetery shrouded in smoke and cordite mist.

Stevenson signaled the team leaders again.

The UFORCE troopers dropped into the courtyard and began the second phase of the operation.

THE SPECIAL-EFFECTS TEAM struck first. While the rest of the UFORCE soldiers covered them, they spread out, carrying their SNPE "porcupine" rifles.

The rifles were part of UFORCE's soft-kill arsenal, weapons designed to disable the enemy as quickly as possible.

A narrow canister of gas was mounted on top of the snout-like barrel. It had a thin hose running from the canister to a dart-shaped projectile that was fixed onto the end of the barrel.

Except for the slight thumping sound it made when the trigger was pulled, it worked like a silent spear gun.

The SNPE-wielding troops lined up outside the walls and nosed the spiny barrels forward. In unison they pulled the triggers and pierced the walls.

After each thump there was a low hissing sound made by the canister as it emptied its contents into the rooms just behind the walls.

The cosmic cocktail flooded the interiors quickly, spreading the aromaless mixture of diazepam, ketamine and a tincture of conventional BZ gas.

It was designed for total disorientation and instant dispersion. During the first thirty seconds it crept up on the victim and then suddenly took hold of them, making it impossible to speak and instilling an overall sense of panic.

Two minutes of exposure caused a wide range of unpredictable reactions. Most subjects who were gassed experienced amnesiac conditions or temporary paralysis. Some were knocked out instantly. Now and then, depending upon their body chemistry, some of the subjects died.

The SNPE gas was one of the more exotic weapons developed for UFORCE by the late Dr. Schyler. It had proved to be wildly successful. Without the disabling gas, Goddard's psy-war ops would never had achieved the same devastating effects.

Thirty seconds after the SNPE troops began their chemical

assault, an elegant-looking woman in a backless dress staggered out the front door. Jewelry dripped down her neck into her plunging bodice, and there were diamond wristlets on both hands.

Her long black hair had a silver streak down one side that added to her exotic appeal. She was in her thirties and she was absolutely stunning. So stunning that Stevenson stared at her for several seconds while deciding whether to kill her or not.

RACQUEL STRALINA STEPPED out into the open air wondering how the dizziness had come upon her so fast. Her lungs felt full of harsh smoke, and she had trouble breathing. It didn't make sense to her. She hadn't smoked anything.

True, the air inside had been full of smoke from cigars and cannabis, but that was customary at these affairs.

Stralina shook her head and took several deep breaths of air, feeling that she was going to faint at any second.

Sacred mother! she thought when she looked out onto the courtyard and saw the guards. The pool of blood gathering around their heads was thick and spreading. For a moment she thought she could almost smell the blood, a coppery scent that drifted heavy in the air.

Then she saw them. The black-clad demons stared at her with long dead eyes. An assortment of weapons dangled from shoulder harnesses and leather holsters. Long knives were strapped to their thighs.

There was something awful about their faces, a primitive and predatory quality that promised no mercy. She felt as if she'd been dropped into a wolf pack. The same pack that had struck in the courtyard.

She looked again and they were gone.

Stralina leaned back against the wall and put her hand to her forehead in an attempt to focus and contain her thoughts. She wondered if someone had slipped something into her drink.

One overwhelming thought won out. She had to run from this dark place. And she had to do it now.

But the future belonged to the man standing in front of her, a large man who dwarfed the dark shapes around him.

He wore a mask of death. A dark green stripe smeared across his earth-stained camouflaged face. Cold black eyes piercing her.

But then the man smiled and reached out for her.

Even as she felt his arm circling around her throat and his hand pulling back on her chin, she sensed that she was in no danger from him. If he was one of the men responsible for the death of the guards, then he could have very easily killed her by now.

Instead he held her in a steely grip that permitted absolutely no movement. He cupped her chin and forced her head back so she was looking at a million pinpoint stars in the sky.

"Do not resist," he said. His lips were close to her neck, and as he spoke she felt his warm breath on her skin.

A moment later she felt a sting in the side of her neck as if an insect had jabbed her. She fell suddenly. The last thing she was aware of were his arms under her shoulders as he dragged her away.

STEVENSON HANDED HER over to a UFORCE trooper who dragged her away from the house and planted her against the wall.

Then he holstered the silver-handled MicroBio inoculator gun, as it was so precisely called by the CIA when its existence was revealed up in the MKULTRA hearings.

The head of the Agency's testimony exposed the CIA's thirty years of dabbling with mind-control technologies that ranged from radio hypnosis to a good old-fashioned mickey that was slipped into the drink of an unsuspecting target. The MicroBio inoculator gun, or MBG, was a totally silent pistol that was powered by a magazine-shaped battery pack. It could fire a variety of tiny darts that carried everything from lethal poisons to simple knockout drugs.

It left almost no mark at all, a trace that could only be de-

tected by the most sophisticated forensic labs, and that was
only if investigators knew what they were looking for.

Several of the UFORCE soldiers carried the MBGs with
them in case they needed to put anyone down suddenly and
safely.

"Here it comes, Captain."

Stevenson looked up where Chet Matthews was pointing.
The Borealis was making its approach. "Get ready," he
shouted to his men. "The show's on."

A LOUD ROAR FILLED the skies above the courtyard as the Borealis descended.

It hovered above the main house and lowered the ramp onto
the rooftop.

Six short figures in dull gray suits climbed onto the roof,
then jumped to the ground. As they headed for the doors, the
Borealis drifted over the courtyard so it could be seen by
everyone inside the house.

A beam shot out from the bottom of the ship. It was an
electromagnetic pulse that instantly knocked out the power in
all of the buildings and shut off the lights.

Then the light show began. The phased sequence of pulsing
lights on the bottom of the Borealis craft flickered on and off
and bathed the courtyard in brilliant green, red and bright yellow colors.

From inside the main house several faces appeared at the
windows to look up at the ship. Many of them had been in-
toxicated even before the gas attack began. Now they were
even more disoriented. But even through the drug-induced haze
they recognized the familiar shape of the triangular UFO that
was often seen drifting above the Mexican skies.

It began making a loud electronic humming sound that gradually increased in strength until the windows began to shudder.

While the occupants of the house were distracted by the
hypnotic drone of the extraterrestrial craft, the Grays began
slipping through the doors and drifting among the guests of
Bastian Dominguez.

Gradually it dawned on the captive audience that visitors were in their midst.

Men and women were sitting at their tables, heads in their hands. Some of them were crying, while some were laughing. A good many of them were spread out on the floor, partially paralyzed and trapped in their own temporary hell. But even they could see the Grays walking among them.

Now and then one of the half-conscious men would try to reach toward the aliens as if he couldn't believe what he was seeing and had to touch it. The UFORCE Grays easily eluded them, except for one man who was suffering more from drunkenness than delusions.

Bellowing with rage, the man rose from the floor and lumbered toward one of the Grays, stepping over the human debris on the floor. His hands reached out for the alien in a slow-motion tackle.

The Gray calmly studied the attacker's approach, then waved a compact light gun toward him. Click. A strobing flash erupted from the lens of the gun and dazzled the man's eyes. He staggered backward as if he'd been hit by a sledgehammer.

The Gray continued flashing the device at him, using it like a leash to control the man's movements. The pulsed light beams battered away at the man's eyes until it overloaded his nervous system and sent him into an epileptic seizure. He sprawled on top of a table, shaking as if he were being electrocuted.

Then he slid down in a pile of broken wineglasses and fell into a catatonic daze.

The Gray took no more notice of him.

He joined the succession of other Grays walking to the back of the long palatial room. They stopped and formed a silent circle around the table where Bastian Dominguez had been sitting with the leading members of the Sonora syndicate.

With bleary eyes, the elite drug merchants watched the reptilian creatures grab Bastian Dominguez by the arms and effortlessly lift him out of his chair.

Compared to the drug lord's massive girth, the Grays

seemed like slender, stick-like beings incapable of physically moving him. But they moved with such speed and grace that it seemed to all the witnesses that Dominguez were floating out of the room.

When the Grays escorted Dominguez from the main house out to the front gate, the SNPE squad took up their positions again and fired several more rounds of gas into the rooms. The show was over and they didn't want anyone to interfere with the cleanup activities.

Within thirty seconds every man and woman in the house was unconscious.

Outside the gates the black manta craft waited for the procession of Grays who marched Dominguez toward the ramp. After the alien detachment led him up the stairs and secured the prisoner, Stevenson climbed up the ramp.

It was time to attend to the passenger.

The other UFORCE commandos carried or dragged the bodies of the slain guards through the gates to the black helicopters that waited for them outside. Three of the choppers were slated to ferry away the dead, silent hearses that would attend to their task unseen. The funeral services would be brief. The men who fell in the courtyard would be dumped into remote canyons where the creatures of the wild would welcome them back into the food chain.

And in the morning there would be no sign of the bodyguards or the drug baron who'd expected them to protect his home.

One by one the guests would recover from the SNPE gas. Some of them would have a total blackout about the evening, but others would have vague recollections of what happened to them. Still others would have vivid impressions of the strange encounter that began with the sighting of the ship as it hovered above the desert fortress and bombarded them with light. They would remember the bizarre gray beings that had come to take Dominguez away.

Though many of the guests would initially keep the incident to themselves, word would get out eventually. The syndicate brokers would report the event to their police and intelligence contacts.

And together they would try to piece together the greatest mystery of the evening...where had all the money gone?

At the moment it was being handled by Stevenson's men. The UFORCE troopers quickly broke into the vault room beneath Dominguez's private quarters and helped themselves to satchels that were full of bundled American dollars.

Under the eyes of Matthews they carried the treasure trove out to one of the empty helicopters and piled the satchels inside. By the time they loaded all of the currency into the cabin, UFORCE was several million dollars richer.

But there was a greater fortune to be had. And the key to that fortune lay within the mind of Dominguez, who would soon wake to find himself in another world.

The world of Colonel Goddard and UFORCE.

BASTIAN DOMINGUEZ WAS fully conscious but couldn't move an inch.

He was strapped to a cold metal chair bolted to the floor of what looked like an airborne medic station. His sleeves had been cut, and there was a fresh needle mark in his arm.

The Mexican syndicate chief could tell that he was in some kind of high-speed craft because of the loud droning and the constant up-and-down motion that it made.

Other than the stainless-steel counters and locked cabinets in front of him, there was little he could see.

Straps secured his arms and legs, and there were metal lock plates clamped down on his fingers. He could move his neck slightly.

He felt an emotion that had been absent from his life for longer than he could remember. Fear. Whoever had gone to all this trouble had done so for a reason. And whoever was behind it was obviously more powerful than the combined strength of the Sonora syndicate.

They'd taken him from his home. He remembered that much. And then there was the ship in the courtyard that everyone had been talking about. The spaceship. The UFO. He'd been too tired to get up to see for himself, but he remembered the reflections of the lights as they bombarded the house.

And then he remembered the gray beings. Impossible, he thought. They couldn't have been real. He was a sophisticated man and he didn't believe in God or otherworldy beings. He only believed in power.

The door behind him clicked open and two men stepped into the room, slowly walking around so he could see them. And then he realized he was in the hands of one of the most lethal powers on earth.

"Colonel Goddard," he said.

Goddard nodded at him. "Señor Dominguez," he said. His measured voice held no anger. No kindness, either.

Dominguez shifted his gaze to the other man, the tall captain he'd seen in Goddard's company so many times before. This was the colonel's fixer. The man who could arrange shipments of weapons for the Sonora syndicate. A man who could also sell the services of the hard-faced men who knew how to use those weapons.

Seeing the captain reassured Dominguez. True, he was in the hands of dangerous men. But he also knew the captain to be a reasonable man. "Where are we?" he asked.

"The ship," Goddard answered.

"What ship?"

"My ship. The one that will be seen all across your country tonight. The ship that took you away."

The bound man nodded. "It's all coming back now," he said. "Those gray beings—everyone thought they were aliens. But they were your people." His eyes sought confirmation from his captor.

Goddard remained silent just long enough for Dominguez to worry.

"Weren't they?"

"Yes," Goddard said, permitting a slash of a smile to appear on his face. "But is it so hard to believe that we are in league with them? Many of your countrymen, and mine, think so.

After all, we are the people they would naturally seek out. People with power.''

"And money," Dominguez stated. "I realize you must have taken it. Where is it?''

"Where it will do most good.''

"That money belongs to some important people in my country. This includes patrons in the intelligence services. I'm sure they will understand a mistake has been made. As long as you return the money, you need not fear any retribution.''

The colonel shrugged. "Under ordinary circumstances that could be arranged. Unfortunately we are forced to do this. The money won't be returned.''

Anger colored the man's face. Even strapped into the chair, he summoned a ferocious gaze. On civilians it might have an effect, but the military men ignored the bravado.

"That's just the way it is," Goddard said. "The sooner you understand that, the sooner we can proceed.''

Dominguez strained at his bonds and shouted, "The entire forces of Mexico will come after you! Do you understand? The entire country!''

Goddard nodded. "Might as well make it two.''

"What do you mean?''

"I already have the armed forces of the United States after me. Special-operations teams. FBI. Justice Department task forces.''

"Then what do you want from me?''

Goddard nodded at the captain. The tall man unlocked one of the cabinets and withdrew a small rack of stoppered glass tubes. He set it on the counter, then took a syringe from one of the drawers.

"There's no need for this," Dominguez said. "If the money is that important to you…''

"It's not just *that* money," Goddard said.

"It isn't? Then why—?''

"It's the rest of your accounts," Goddard stated. "We'll need the numbers and passwords for your Swiss accounts, as well as the false identities you used to open them. Same goes for the Panamanian assets. Captain Stevenson will take down the information. I truly regret using the drug, but I'm afraid without the chemical incentives, you wouldn't reveal them to us."

"How do you know about those accounts?" Dominguez demanded. "They were hidden."

"Yes," Goddard said. "But not very well. Now let's get on with it."

Stevenson stepped forward, gripped the man's arm and then prepared to inject him with the compound that had been developed by the Agency for interrogation of defectors.

It was the closest thing to a truth serum ever created. It had also been outlawed for use by any branch of the U.S. government, but since UFORCE was no longer a part of that government, Goddard had no compunction about using it. Although the drug successfully released all inhibitions and memories in the subject, it was also a one-time, one-way compound that permanently damaged the memory core and left the subject a vegetable.

Dominguez looked up at Goddard. "You won't get away with this, Colonel. I swear. I'll never forget it."

"Actually," Stevenson said as he injected him with the drug, "you will." He sat across from him and hit a button on a small digital recorder. Then he began the interrogation that would empty every last thought from Dominguez.

ONE HOUR LATER Goddard was directing the Borealis to cross the border into the neighboring state of Chihuahua when the bad news arrived.

Although the mission in Sonora went off exactly as expected, word was coming in that the Ark Springs operation had literally blown up in their face. Three trucks and the troops who were being transported inside them were out of action for good. The ghost-town staging area had been taken, and the weapons cache was now in enemy hands.

First the New Mexico base had been overrun and now this. Two strategic defeats, one right after the other.

He needed to regroup. But first he needed to refuel at the underground base they'd constructed in the middle of one of Chihuahua's largest ranch lands.

From there they would head back to the U.S. and begin the disinformation campaign that would lead the COG and Justice Department tasks forces in all the wrong directions. Unless he unleashed a wave of UFORCE sightings to get them chasing their tails, it wouldn't be long before they zeroed in on his remaining bases in the Southwest.

Another man might have reconsidered his actions. With all the might of the U.S. covert forces coming after him, Goddard could easily have folded. It would be simple enough for him to go abroad, take up a new name and live a life of luxury.

But he couldn't ignore the primeval call that shouted from the very core of his being. From deep inside his heart, Goddard knew that a seasoned soldier like himself wasn't destined to leave the country.

He was destined to lead it.

10

San Luis Valley, Colorado

Mack Bolan sat in the copilot's seat of the Nightfox helicopter as it flew high above the sunstruck crop circles on J. D. Freeman's farm just outside the town of Ballard Mills.

The Executioner was looking down on the elegantly cut furrows through the lens of a high-tech video camera.

Even though it was still early in the afternoon, when most people would be working, a fair-size crowd was wandering across the site. Now and then they looked up at the Nightfox. Some of them snapped photos or videotaped the helicopter before turning their attention back to the crop circle. A lot more of them waved up at the soldier, practically jumping up and down like game-show contestants trying to look memorable enough to earn their spot on television.

He waved back, playing out his civilian role as a reporter in search of a story. They'd landed near the field a few times already to interview some of the curiosity seekers. By now the helicopter was as much a part of the show as the crop circles themselves. Everyone knew, or thought they knew, that a documentary film crew was on the scene.

The Nightfox flew over the hilly terrain on the north side of the crop circles, then looped back along the stream that bordered the enigmatic emblems carved into the field.

The Nightfox weapons platforms had been removed from the chopper, and the side panels on the exterior of the cabin proclaimed it to be the property of Ground Force Productions,

Inc., a Colorado-based video-production company that produced several military-oriented cable-television programs.

Although the programs that aired were of extremely high quality, GFP also had another reason for existing. Many of the people who worked for the globe-trotting company were military or Agency operatives who used it as a cover for intelligence or surveillance operations.

It was a perfect cover, mainly because it was one of the most profitable enterprises the government had been involved with. Many of the operatives were experts on military history, and if pressed, they could put on a convincing show.

GFP did several programs on Special Forces training and peacekeeping operations along with their bread-and-butter documentaries about wartime operations.

GFP also did some investigative programs now and then, including the current feature that Bolan was allegedly attached to, "The Circle Game: the Strange Connection between Crop Circles, Cattle Mutilations, and Alien Visitations."

"Camera works better if you put film in it," Melissa Rogers said. The pilot of the Nightfox nodded toward the state-of-the-art piece of equipment in Bolan's hand. "You getting tired of playing Edward R. Murrow yet?"

"Just giving them something to look at," Bolan answered, waving down at a trio of ten-year-olds who were jumping up and down in the field and trying to get his attention.

"Let's see," she said. "They've got you. They've got the crop circle, and they've got Old MacDonald down there." She nodded her head toward J. D. Freeman's lean rangy figure as he strolled calmly near the fence line, watching his field get overrun by crop-circle chasers. "What more could they want?"

"Maybe a real crop circle," Bolan said.

"We'd all be better off if it was."

"Without a doubt," the soldier said. "Until that happens, we're stuck with the UFORCE bit. You've got to hand it to them. They sure know how to bring out the marks."

"Including us," Rogers said. "I've seen enough crop circles

on this tour to last me a lifetime. Although this one's almost pretty when you think of it.''

"Yeah, almost," Bolan said, looking down at the maze below them. It had a vague Stonehenge look to it, with a round pattern of circles capped by shapes that could be altar stones. The long diagonal staffs that sliced through them looked like musical notes. Several smaller circles flanked the main design, as if they were orbiting planets or maybe spaceships.

Bolan wondered what it was about the crop circles that made them so effective. The one below them was similar to at least thirty other crop circles that had recently appeared across the southwestern states. Some of them went unreported. Some of them, like this one, created a carnival atmosphere.

There were slight variations among the circles, but one thing remained constant. They all seemed to be saying something profound, offering equations that solved the riddle of the universe or alien pictograms that supposedly were greetings from Arcturus. In effect they were nothing more than large-scale Rorschach blots that could mean whatever you wanted them to mean, since no one on Earth could prove you wrong.

The Freeman's farm circle would have been just like all the other ones the helicopter had flown over, Bolan thought, if not for one crucial difference. The unseen hand of UFORCE had finally revealed itself.

And it had revealed itself to none other than the farmer who stood below them, the stone-faced and laconic J. D. Freeman.

"Give me the word whenever you want to go down," she said. "The nose camera's got everybody and their brother on tape. Any UFORCE renegades down there, we got them dead to rights. Got close-ups of their back molars if you want them."

"Make one more run," Bolan said. "Then I'll go down and say hello to the crop stalkers."

The soldier glanced over at the GFP pilot as he confidently worked the controls of the specially-designed recon chopper. She was a lot more interesting to watch than anything in the field below.

Before her current stint with GFP, Rogers had flown combat missions in the Gulf and in Central America and in a few other places she hadn't mentioned during their premission briefing.

She was a hard-core pilot with short black hair, trim figure and a skeptical gaze that always seemed to be saying, "You've got to be kidding." That attitude helped her come back to the studio with the kind of in-depth, revealing interviews that might have escaped more timid reporters. But after surviving wars where people were shooting for real, surviving the ratings wars was a piece of cake. She was one of the reasons for GFP's success in the documentary arena.

Rogers pulled back on the controls and took the chopper up for one last figure-eight pattern over the crop circles. From this height the laser-carved furrows looked like a combination of giant musical notes and Aryan thunderbolts.

"That's it for me," she said. "Show's over. We keep this up, we'll be running out of fuel."

"Okay," he said. "Take me down. I'll see what I can find."

He loaded a tape into the video camera as she flew the helicopter to a level spot on the field that was clear enough and solid enough to make a landing. Bolan knew there already were several trained operatives walking around, filming the crowd, as well as the circle, but he figured he might turn up a face the others missed.

The operatives on the ground were looking for possible UFORCE troops reconning the area, who might even be taping them at the same time. After all, UFORCE had made a mistake and it was only logical for them to come back and arrange damage control. Until now the actual method of UFORCE operations had been a closely kept secret, known only to Goddard's people and the people trying to catch them. That might all change now. The UFORCE witnesses might become more aggressive...like slow-talking J. D. Freeman.

"I'll be back in an hour to pick you up," Rogers said when she landed the Nightfox.

Bolan nodded, ducked and jumped out of the cabin. He crouched low until he was past the range of the rotor wash.

He slung the video camera strap over his shoulder and then headed out to do some spot interviews with the crowd.

Every now and then the soldier used the zoom lens to take a look at Freeman. He was still lingering by his vantage point just outside the fence. Every time he looked his way, Bolan saw the laconic farmer glancing back at him with a stone-faced gaze.

The man didn't miss much, Bolan thought. Freeman knew that an undercover operation was in full swing. He just wasn't sure who all the players were. And neither was Bolan.

Bolan swept the camera lens across the field as he walked through the maze like a penitent reliving the stations of the cross. He was filming for real this time, just in case any players that he didn't know showed up on the scene.

J. D. FREEMAN WATCHED the silhouette of the helicopter dwindle as it flew back toward Ballard Mills.

Good riddance, he thought. It'd be a hell of a lot quieter around here without the blades chopping through the air. Quiet enough to think his way out of the maze he'd found himself caught up in.

He didn't ask for any of this to happen, but it literally fell from the sky and dropped right into his lap and now he was stuck with it.

The crop circles appeared overnight in a field of tall grass across the road from his farmhouse. Even before daybreak the news had spread, and now everyone in the town of Ballard Mills knew all about it.

The area was prosperous enough to support a small school, a department store, a couple of grocery stores, a bookshop and café, and the surest sign of civilization, a videotape rental store.

There were approximately two thousand people who actually lived within the town limits of Ballard Mills, and thanks to the highly developed grapevine, nearly every one of them heard about the alien invasion before the morning was out.

By one in the afternoon it seemed that nearly half of the population was out on the county line road in search of aliens, angels or black helicopters. Pickup trucks, cars and a couple of tractors were parked on both sides of the road bisecting several acres of tall grass that belonged to a semiretired rancher named J. D. Freeman.

Freeman stood at the side of the road in blue jean overalls with a pair of leather work gloves stuffed in the back pocket, the same ones he had with him every day of the year. He wore steel-toed boots and a light brown work shirt with the sleeves rolled up to his elbows. He rested a gnarled, weathered hand on top of a fence post as he stood by and watched the show.

He did his best to maintain a look of mild amusement on his face while his neighbors treaded through the fields in small groups of twos and threes. Sometimes an entire family came out to the farm, blazing a trail to the tentless circus that had come to town.

He could have charged admission if he was so inclined, and it would have made him a small fortune. But it wasn't in his nature to profit from something that fell out of the blue like this. Freeman didn't regard the circles in his field as his. It would be like charging someone to see a rainbow. A phenomenon of this magnitude belonged to the world. And as far as he was concerned, they could have it. Besides, there was a sinister element about the circles that none of the thrill seekers could even guess.

If he had his way, they would never know about it. The last thing he needed was to become a laughingstock of the county. Nor did he want to create any risk at all for his wife, who was still in the dark about what really happened.

So he acted the part that everyone expected him to portray. Just a down-home farmer with callused hands, a kind heart and a devil-may-care attitude about the mysterious designs in his field.

Messages from the stars.

Signals from the long-lost space brothers.

The brand of the devil was more like it, he thought.

Christ, he thought, people were so gullible when they wanted to hear that they were special, that an extraterrestrial race had traveled all the way to Earth to contact them, and instead of landing on the White House lawn or at least picking up the phone and saying hello, they traveled out in the middle of nowhere to carve a bunch of laser-guided squiggles in Freeman's field.

Grown men and women trampled the tall grass like kids on an Easter-egg hunt. Freeman could hear their excited voices talking about aliens.

Not one of them looked back as they hurried toward the strange and inexplicable phenomenon that materialized sometime during the night on Freeman's farm. Not one of them really looked close at the worry lines on Freeman's face. They were too blinded with fairy dust to see the dark and dangerous reality before them.

The cars kept coming throughout the afternoon. Every few minutes another vehicle pulled over to the side of the road to dislodge a fresh stream of sight-seers. They would look out at the field, then look over at Freeman and hurry to his side.

They were always full of questions. He gave the same answers to anyone who asked.

Yes, they had permission to go in the field and look for themselves.

Of course, he would always add after they started to hurry away, they had to enter at their own risk. He couldn't guarantee that they wouldn't catch their heels on a gopher hole, get whisked away on a flying saucer or fall on their damn-fool head if they climbed one of the trees on the edge of the field to get a better look.

No, he told them, he didn't know what caused the crop circles. Until now he'd only seen them on television shows and that was mostly in England, though like everyone else, he heard rumors that more and more crop circles were popping up in the Southwest, particularly New Mexico and Colorado—especially this part of Colorado. They had NORAD in Cheyenne Mountain, so why the hell not have an alien base in the south?

Alien bases. That was a new one for him. He didn't know

where the rumor started, but several of the people were already talking about some base that was supposedly hidden around here.

It was funny, he thought. Many of the visitors to his farm had practically the same reaction. After the initial shock wore off, they voiced their disbelief that anything of cosmic importance could happen here in Ballard Mills. Then they would explain that, even so, they were open-minded enough to entertain the possibility that the aliens had come to make a statement.

Next they'd tell him how they heard about it, how everyone in town knew about it ever since the sheriff came out in the morning to question Freeman and look at the field for himself.

Then they'd ask more questions.

Did he know that neighbors for miles around had reported seeing strange lights in the sky last night? And how come he didn't see anything?

Because he was in bed at the time, he told them. After all, he had to get up with the cows, didn't he? And yes, he'd heard about ranchers and farmers across the country making calls to the sheriff's department in the middle of the night but he certainly wasn't among them. He told everyone the same story, that all he knew was that the crop circles weren't there yesterday but they sure as hell were there today.

Though he considered many of the townsmen his friends, he didn't trust any of them enough to tell them the real story, the one that he'd told County Sheriff Eugene Sanger who came out to investigate in the dark hours of the morning. It just might get them killed if they knew the truth.

So he played the country bumpkin. No one thought twice about whatever story he told them. In these parts Freeman was a man beyond reproach.

Everyone in Ballard Mills knew in the bottom of their hearts that he was incapable of perpetrating a hoax. The one-time mayor and Army veteran was a straight shooter, a salt-of-the-earth type whose family had lived here for generations. He had a reputation as a fair-minded but no-nonsense type of guy who didn't suffer fools but was friendly enough unless you crossed him.

Married to his wife of thirty-two years, he was in his late fifties with two grown children who'd moved away long ago. They were through with college and had jobs and children of their own. The grandchildren came out to spend part of the summers in Ballard Mills and sometimes they'd have an extended winter vacation. He did his best to give them an appreciation of the land and the generations of ancestors who'd worked it before him. In the back of his mind he thought that maybe one day his son or grandson would come back home to carry on the tradition. The land would be here waiting for them whenever they wanted.

Freeman had downsized his operation these past few years and become something of a gentleman farmer. He kept a small dairy farm close to the one-hundred-year-old farmhouse he'd restored board by board until it looked as strong and sturdy as the day it was first built.

Freeman didn't need the income from the dairy operation, but he needed to carry on the farming for a much deeper reason. It was in his blood. Besides, in these crazy times it was prudent to have a self-sufficient place.

He was letting a lot of the other acreage go wild, which made it a perfect canvas for the crop-circle artists who branded his property.

If only it had stopped there, Freeman thought.

He shook his head and looked up at the clear afternoon sky, almost as if he expected to see a saucer scooting across the clouds.

Aliens.

Crop circles.

Nothing but a hoax, he thought. And a dangerous one at that.

After sitting up half the night with a rifle in his hands, he'd come back out to the field after dawn and walked up and down the crop circles. The intersecting paths carved out of the overgrown fields looked like strips of freshly mown grass...except for a scorched burning scent that lingered in the air. It was the unsettling scent of brimstone.

One part of him appreciated the neat and intricate designs under his feet, but the other part wondered about their real reason for coming here in the first place. And he'd scoured nearly every foot of that damn circle to see if they left anything behind.

If so, he knew they would return and it wouldn't be just to add a few finishing touches to the drawings.

He climbed up the wooded hillside for a better look. It wasn't high enough to get a total picture of the shapes, but he could make out the symmetry of the circles and the links that connected them.

It almost looked like a blueprint that someone had carved from above.

Someone, he thought. Not something.

It wasn't the product of any off-world race.

At least this particular circle wasn't alien in origin. The things he'd seen in the back fields hadn't come from some other solar system, although in a way, he wished they really had. If that was the case, life would be a lot simpler for him and a lot less dangerous.

Despite what he told the others, Freeman had seen the lights in the sky. Seen them in black and white. And red and green. The events were still fresh in his mind. At least what he could recall of them...

AT THREE O'CLOCK in the morning Freeman found himself sitting upright in his bed, yanked out of sleep by a whooshing sound that cut through his dreams like a shock wave. The strange unearthly clamor quieted the usual nocturnal sounds that a man got used to out in the country. Something different was out there in the middle of the night.

He looked at his wife, Rebecca, but she was still sleeping soundly. Her long grayish-brown hair was spread out on the pillow, and she was wrapped in the cocoon of a homemade quilt.

Freeman placed his hand on her shoulder, but she didn't stir. Good. No need for her to worry.

He slipped out of bed and dressed quickly, then walked gently down the creaking staircase to the darkened front room. He hooked his finger into the side of the drapes and peered out through the picture window.

Lights danced in the sky. Glowing spheres. Long pulsing bars of light. The blinking lights were followed by an almost umbrella-like burst of multicolored lights showering down from the sky like fireworks.

When the afterimage of the fireworks faded away, two circular spheres weaved up and down and circled the field.

Then the lights blinked out and the sky was dark once again.

Freeman stood at the window wondering if this was all part of a dream and he'd just woken up. But his senses were wide-awake and so was he.

Something had been out there. Maybe it still was.

He put on his denim jacket and slipped out the side door of the farmhouse, carrying a rifle in one hand and a flashlight in the other.

He had experience in combat and knew how to move so he wouldn't be seen. He also knew the lay of the land better than anyone else possibly could.

As he stepped outside into the chill air he realized it probably wasn't the smartest thing in the world to do. Or the easiest.

But he wasn't the kind of man to turn away and let someone else take care of business for him. For good or worse, he took things into his own hands.

Freeman drifted behind the barn and made his way down to the fast-running stream that flowed across his property toward the county road. The sound of the water provided good cover for his approach. There were several smooth boulders in the middle of the stream and a lot of small waterfalls so it was always splashing and gurgling and sounding as if someone were walking through it.

So that's exactly what he did.

He stuffed the flashlight into his jacket pocket, held his rifle in a two-handed grip and then walked through the stream, crouching down so that his body was hidden by the banks on both sides.

Tall trees and brush flanked the stream, creating a screen of shadows every step of the way.

The farther he got away from the house, the more he found himself clutching the rifle in his hand, reassured by the solid cold metal. He didn't expect to run into any serious trouble. But he wasn't going to run away, either. Not on his own land. Besides, this was just a short jaunt, a recon of his own field. No one would notice him.

When the stream reached the road, it flowed through a metal-reinforced gully. The gully cored a five-foot-high passage through the embankment beneath the blacktop.

The cold dark water rose above his knees as he sloshed through the gully. It soaked his skin like a blanket of ice weighing down his movements.

He emerged from the other side and stayed in a low crouch, moving his feet with a stalker's gait as he followed the stream.

That's when he saw them.

Black shapes were flying in the night. The silhouettes were barely visible against the dark sky, but their constant motion was hard to miss. There were several of the shapes swooping around up there, hardly making a sound as they revolved around a much larger craft.

Helicopters.

Just helicopters. He'd flown in enough of them during his government-sponsored tour of Southeast Asia to recognize them.

But these were silent choppers, quieter than anything he'd ever heard. The silent black helicopters really existed. Just as all the wacko theories said, black choppers were haunting the Midwest and the proof was right in front of his eyes.

To see the helicopters by themselves would have been more than enough. But to see them accompanying a mother ship was almost more than he could believe, even though it was right in front of his eyes.

For some reason he couldn't get a fix on the shape of the largest ship. At times it seemed to be a long cigar-shaped craft, but then, just when he was certain of its dimensions, it suddenly changed into a saucer shape.

A ring of multicolored lights flicked on and off from the portal holes on the bottom of the craft. The stunning display had a hypnotic effect on him, making him stand perfectly still in the water until it went dark again.

He could just barely see the outline of it now, a black bat-wing shape that hovered high above the tree line. It seemed to have a dull black finish. Or maybe it was a shade of deep blue. Whatever it was, it perfectly matched the color of the sky above the UFO.

Bright beams of light suddenly shot out from the bottom of the craft and sliced down through the overgrown field.

Freeman stood there watching the daggers of light as long as he could. Then he had to cover his face to shield his eyes from the increasingly brilliant illumination. He lowered his head for almost a full minute, using his peripheral vision to watch the surging flashes of light.

When the lights finally stopped, he looked up again. There in the fading light he saw *them* moving about.

It paralyzed him where he stood, and for the first time in his life he had no idea what to do. Until now he'd survived everything the world could throw at him. But now he was facing something beyond the world.

Gray figures were walking through the field, moving back and forth in exactly the same area where the lights had been aimed.

Aliens. Just like all of the reports in the supermarket tabloids. He'd seen those same faces looking out at him from the racks at the checkout counters. Usually the aliens had one arm draped over the President's shoulders, and there was always a headline above it announcing some kind of secret pact between the U.S. and the extraterrestrials.

But this was real, even though it had the feeling of a dream.

The aliens had begun to spread out through the field, almost as if they weren't too worried about being seen by anyone. Or maybe they even wanted to be seen, he thought.

It reminded him of a scouting party that was fanning out in all directions while it looked for the enemy.

Enemy. He wondered if he fit that description in their eyes. He scanned the fields on both sides of the stream to see if any of them had outflanked him.

A moment later he felt a huge wave of relief pour through him when headlights speared the darkness from a few miles away. He would not have to face these creatures alone.

Farther up in the hills he could see lights blinking on in houses that had been totally dark a moment ago. The alarm was spreading.

Good, he thought. The more witnesses the better.

As the figures drew closer, he figured it might be wise to pull back toward his side of the road. There was more cover there.

Before he could move a single step, he heard something thrashing the woods behind him.

He spun around and saw the gray figure stepping through the brush at the side of the bank. There was just enough time for him to take in the dark eyes, the smooth, nearly featureless face and the reptilian fingers before he swung the rifle.

It was an instinctive act that he was powerless to stop. And it was all over in a split second. His left hand levered the rifle barrel back toward him while his right hand snapped the stock forward.

The rifle butt smashed into the creature's chin and lifted it off its feet. As the thing's head snapped back, all he could think of was that it sure as hell was built a lot more solid than it looked.

The thing landed on the edge of the bank and slid into the water, floating at Freeman's feet.

He almost screamed at the sight of the nightmarish body

looking blankly up at the stars, its clawlike fingers curled up like a dead bug. Only his training kept him silent.

What if it was dead? he thought. What if they'd finally decided to make contact with the primitive race on earth, judging that they'd finally evolved to the point where contact would be beneficial for both sides? They'd come all that way for such a noble purpose only to have Freeman kill the first one he saw.

He reached down and grabbed the thing's arm, then tugged it to the side of the bank.

One of its hands caught on the muddy slope and it sank back into the water, floating facedown.

Freeman made a wild grab for the creature and hooked his hand around its neck, yanking it out of the water and right out of its skin.

The face came off in his hand. It flipped back and forth in the moonlight and dripped water like a caught fish.

Streaks of blood cascaded down his wrist when he held it aloft like a scalp. Dead black eyes looked back at him, shining darkly in the moonlight. The gill-shaped breathing slits were stained red.

He looked down at the thing at his feet and to his relief saw that it was an unconscious man lying there. His face was bloodied but he was alive.

Freeman crouched lower for a closer look at the human being. The man's eyes were closed as if he were sleeping…thanks to the narcotic effect of Freeman's hardwood rifle stock.

Now that he was up close he could see that it was a clean-shaven man with a short military haircut. Gouts of blood had splattered up from his mouth when his teeth clacked together. A halo of the thick dark liquid had gathered at his lips, enough for him to drown in it if he was left that way.

Humans after all, he thought. What had he been thinking all along? What else could it be but a hoax?

Yes, he thought. It was definitely a hoax. But what the hell were they doing out there at his farm?

What did they want from him?

He dragged the man farther up the bank and tilted his head so the blood ran out of his mouth instead of down his throat. The man coughed softly, straining to breathe.

He was alive. And he was deadly. If he woke now, he wouldn't look too kindly on the man who'd nearly taken his head off.

Freeman silently eased himself down the bank and walked back into the river, cleansing his hand and wrist in the cold rushing water.

The farmer held on to the mask for a couple more seconds, while debating whether or not he should keep it. As a trophy it would be proof of what he'd seen out there. But it would also be proof to the visitors that someone else had been in the field beside the costumed "aliens," and they might come after him. Besides, he thought, what the hell could he do with it? Mount it on the wall above the fireplace and tell everyone there was the buck he caught? No, he had to get rid of it. And he had to get away.

He tossed the mask toward the man's head. It slapped wetly against his cheek and then fell to the ground beside him. It looked as harmless as a Halloween mask.

Freeman hurried back to the road and slipped through the gully, then headed back up to his farmhouse. By the time he reached the side door, he saw a solitary headlight sweeping down the road.

It was a pickup truck with a broken headlight on the passenger side. When it stopped in the middle of the road, he recognized the battered old rust bucket that belonged to his nearest neighbor, Clarence Johansson, who'd come here to check out the light show that obviously woke him up. Johansson jumped out of his truck in his typical bullish manner and slammed the door loud enough to wake the dead. Then he stomped off toward Freeman's field to take matters in his hands.

A pair of headlights was approaching from the opposite direction. Freeman didn't recognize the second vehicle when it came to a stop about ten yards away from the pickup truck.

But he was glad for the company. For some reason he felt that nothing bad would happen to him as long as the others were out here.

Then again, he thought, the people who were capable of running that ship probably wouldn't find it too difficult to handle a couple of good old boys who came out to see the lights.

Freeman slipped inside his house and headed straight for the parlor. Keeping the lights off, he held the phone close to his eyes and read the county sheriff's number on the handset label. After tapping in the numbers he was surprised to hear the dispatcher pick up on the first ring.

Dorothy Daniels, the object of affection for most of Ballard Mills's eligible bachelors, recognized Freeman's voice right off and said, "I know, J.D., don't tell me. You saw some crazy lights in the sky. Congratulations. You are our one hundredth caller of the evening. You win the grand—"

"My story's different, Dorothy," he said.

The tone in his voice clued her in immediately. "Hold on, I'm putting you through to the sheriff."

Sheriff Sanger came on the line and said, "What the hell have you got going on out there, J.D.?"

Freeman told him, holding nothing back. Sanger was about the only man in the county he could trust with the truth...and with his life. As he spoke with the sheriff, Freeman went back to the front window to check out the activity there. Another pair of headlights was rolling slowly down the road past his farm and pulling off to the side.

After listening to his account, Sanger stayed silent for several long moments.

"You still there, Sheriff?"

"That I am, J.D. That I am. I'm just thinking things over."

"Well, think a little faster, goddammit," Freeman said. "I've got at least a half dozen of those men in monkey suits sitting across the road from me right now. Add in the black helicopters and the UFO, and there's a regular space armada just waiting to land on me. If it wasn't for the nosy neighbors driving around out there, I don't know if I'd still be talking to you."

"Understood," the sheriff said. "But before we go any further and I step way out on a limb here, I got to make one thing clear. As far as I know, you've never been a drinking man before tonight. Has that changed any?"

"Sober as the day I was born, Sheriff."

"I kind of figured as much, J.D.," the sheriff said. "You just stay right there and don't worry about what you did. Far as I know, there's no law against whapping an alien upside the head, especially if they're torching your field with a bunch of laser beams. I'll be out there as soon as I make a few calls to some people who ought to know about this."

"Who?" Freeman asked, suddenly wondering just how many people would be let in on the secret.

"The people who take care of this sort of thing, J.D. There's a lot more going on in this world than we know about. Or want to."

"Amen to that, Sheriff."

"But it's here and we got to deal with it. Now this group I've got to get in touch with has been looking for this kind of thing and they've got the manpower and the expertise."

"You mean this isn't a one-of-a-kind thing?"

"Not exactly," Sanger said. "We're supposed to be looking out for strange lights in the sky, crop circles and aliens and reporting them up the line to some kind of state and federal task force."

"You mean there really is a government agency chasing after these little green men."

"No, J.D. They're chasing after little gray men, just like the ones out at your place. Far as I know, you're the first one who actually saw beneath the gray mask, J.D. "

It was a dubious honor. Freeman remembered the awe he felt when he'd seen the mother ship and then the Grays prowling through the field. Something like that was a bit beyond the county sheriff's department. "Okay, Sheriff," he said. "I guess you got my permission to do it your way."

Sanger laughed. "It's not a matter of permission, J.D. For the most part, these people come in and do what they got to do and you just stand out of the way."

"I'll do my best, Sheriff," Freeman promised. "Within reason." He hung up the phone aware of only one thing. Whether it was aliens or assassins, he didn't plan on running again.

11

Freeman's Farm, San Luis Valley

The afternoon sun was at its hottest when Freeman noticed a strange face that suddenly caught his attention.

It was the second day after the crop circles had appeared on his property, and interest had died down somewhat. But from time to time small crowds of people still came out to view the phenomenon.

It was a man in his early thirties who seemed more intent on watching the people walking the circle, rather than the circle itself. The guy had blond hair that was slicked back and trimmed so evenly that it seemed to have been cut with the same kind of laser that burned through the field.

Even in jeans and a flannel shirt, which were so new they still had the creases in them, he looked like one of those corporate banker types that Freeman had to deal with now and then when the farm ran into a cash-flow problem, the main problem being that he had no cash.

Those days were far in the past now, thank God, but Freeman still remembered what it was like to deal with men who were just interested in the bottom line. To his kind, people like Freeman were no more than assets or liabilities to be added or discarded as necessary.

The man walked around as if he were breathing a more rarefied air than everyone else, barely able to hide his disdain for the locals who'd come out to see the crop circles. Every now and then when he spoke to some of Freeman's neighbors, the neighbors invariably hurried away.

Not exactly a charmer.

The man suddenly looked his way and caught Freeman studying him. He grinned broadly. It was an empty and soulless gesture, a poor attempt to camouflage himself as a human being.

Freeman felt a shiver of fear run through him, the same thing he'd felt when the alien's fake head came off in his hand.

Maybe this was one of the Grays who crept through the field, he thought. Maybe the blond man was loitering around the crop circle the same way an arsonist came back to examine his handiwork and watch the firemen put out the flames.

Or it could be another one of the government agents who'd been roaming about his place. Some of them were bound to be just as hard as the opposition.

Freeman couldn't tell who was who. All he knew so far was what the sheriff had told him earlier. People would be out here checking out the situation. Some of them would be on the sheriff's side. And some of them just might be working for the other side. The sheriff hadn't come right out and named this other side yet, but he made it clear that the sheriff's department had been brought into the loop and knew that the group existed. And he knew they could be dangerous.

As Freeman stood there watching the man saunter about the field as if it were his own private property, the fear went away. It was immediately replaced by an intense surge of anger that had been building up inside him all day long. This was Freeman's land. He didn't have to put up with this kind of treatment from anybody, friend or foe.

The farmer pushed through the gate and started walking toward the blond man. When he was halfway there he noticed another man in freshly bought jeans and work shirt strolling into the circle. This second man approached the blonde and said a few words. They both looked at Freeman.

Freeman stopped several feet away. "Do I know you?" he demanded.

"No," the blond man said. "I'm new to the area."

"Is that right? Where you staying?" Freeman said. "I know most of the places around here."

The blonde raised his eyebrow, then said, "If you really have to know, maybe you'd better just call up the sheriff and ask him."

"Why should I do that?" the farmer demanded.

"Because we're connected to his office."

"I know most of the deputies," Freeman said. "Even the part-time ones."

"Good," the man said, putting his hand on Freeman's shoulder. He made it look like a friendly gesture, but his grip was hard and his fingers were digging into the tendons. "That's real good. And I'm sure they know you, too." He spoke in a condescending tone, as if he were dealing with a feeble-minded old man. "Now, why don't you just go back over there and hold up that fence post like you've been doing? Leave the rest of the work to us."

Freeman flung the hand off his shoulder. The sudden move surprised the man. So did the strength in the older man's arm. Strength that came from working soil and standing up to people who trampled all over it.

"I'm reporting this to the sheriff."

"Go ahead," the man said. "But first you should realize what I meant before. We don't work for the sheriff. He works for us." The man crossed his arms in front of him, and though he wasn't showing any outward sign of anger, it was there in his eyes.

"Could I see some identification?" Freeman asked.

The man nodded and slipped his hand into the inside pocket of his jacket. He removed a billfold and flipped it open, then held it up to Freeman's eyes for inspection. It was a bit too close for comfort. The official-looking ID said he was Anthony J. Scopece, a special counsel to the Colorado attorney general's office. "Who are you counseling?" Freeman asked.

"Anyone who needs it," he said. "Right now that includes

you, Mr. Freeman. I suggest you take my advice and go back to your post.''

Freeman had an image of being locked away somewhere in a cold and dark room being counseled by this man. ''You know, I think I'll take you up on your other offer,'' he said.

''What's that?''

''To call up the sheriff.''

The man nodded and drew his cellular phone from his outsize pocket on the side of his jeans. He pressed a button that autodialed the sheriff's number and handed the phone to Freeman.

A moment later the farmer heard a woman's familiar voice say, ''Sheriff Sanger's office.''

''This is J. D. Freeman. Let me talk to the sheriff.''

She put him through right away. ''What is it now, J.D.?'' Sanger asked.

Freeman looked at the men who had drifted a few yards away and were talking in low voices, totally unconcerned about him. To them it was as if he no longer existed, just another peasant who'd been put into his place. ''It's about a couple of sharks you sent out to my property here,'' Freeman said, looking at the puffed-up government agents. He described the pair to the sheriff, then finished with a tag both men could hear. ''A couple of real pricks.''

''Ah,'' Sanger said. ''I see you've had the pleasure of their company, too.''

''Afraid so.''

''Well, my advice is to let them be, J.D. This might prove to be a complicated matter.''

''If they stay out here any longer, I might just have to uncomplicate their ass the same way I did that critter last night. I'd like some answers, Sheriff.''

''I can't do much right now,'' Sanger said. ''There's a lot of media inquiries I'm dealing with at the moment. It's got to be handled just the right way or we'll have a hundred more reporters trampling all over your place and we'll never find out what's going on.''

"I'm more concerned with these two federal lunkheads you got out here trampling all over my civil rights."

"When this cools down I'll see what I can do," the sheriff said, hanging up before Freeman could say another word.

The farmer handed the phone back to the blond man.

"Satisfied?" the man asked.

Freeman was about to respond when he caught a flash of movement from his peripheral vision. Another man was moving toward him, someone he'd seen around here for the past couple of days, usually in a black windbreaker and a pair of jeans. It was that reporter for the cable-television show who'd been flying over the fields with the lady pilot. Up close the man had a much sterner look than Freeman remembered.

"Are these men bothering you?" the man asked Freeman.

"They sure as hell are."

"Then they're bothering me, too." The weathered face of the reporter turned to the blond man. "Understand what I'm saying here?"

The blonde quickly reached for his billfold and started to pull it out as if it were a protective talisman. The reporter's hand moved in a blur and caught the man's wrist, turning it slightly in a hard grip.

The Fed had to change his position and bow his head forward to keep his leveraged wrist from breaking in a hard grip. The reporter had done it with an economy of motion and a subtlety that made it impossible for anyone else to guess what was going on. To them it looked like the four of them were just having a casual chat.

"You show that government-issued gate pass once more and you'll eat it, plastic and all," the reporter said. He released the man's grip and stepped back to face both of the covert counselors. "This is supposed to be a discreet operation, gentlemen. We walk softly out here. But the two of you have attracted too much attention. You're off this assignment as of right now."

The blonde protested, but even as he did so, he stepped back a couple of paces and nursed his twisted wrist. "You can't do that," he said. "You don't have the authority. We're with Commander Macauley—"

"I know who you're with," the reporter said. "And I'm taking the authority right now to dismiss you both. If either of you say one more word, I'll have the commander's head in my hands by the end of the day. That's a promise. And I don't think he'll be too happy with you if it gets to that point." With that, the reporter put his hands on both men's shoulders and guided them to the gate.

He came back a half-minute later.

"Sorry about that, Mr. Freeman. This thing had to be put together so fast that they sent some people out who obviously don't belong in the field. At least out in that field anyway. Tell you what, let's you and I have a talk and see what we can work out."

Freeman watched the blond man and his partner walking down the road to their shiny new car and laughed. "Sure thing," he said. "Come on up to the house."

"Not just yet," the reporter said. "It's better to keep a low profile in case anyone's watching. I'll take another look around here until my partner picks me up, but I'll come back as soon as it gets dark. In the meantime you can talk things over with Sheriff Sanger. I understand he's one of the few men in this whole situation that you still trust. Is that correct?"

"Yeah, it is."

"Good. He'll vouch for me. And if you have any more problems like you did with those two jokers, just call him and mention my name. I guarantee those problems will stop immediately."

"It's a deal," Freeman said. "What name should I mention when I call him? I know you're supposed to be a TV guy and all, but I don't recognize you. Not that I watch all that much television anyway."

"Don't worry about it," the man said. "I'm more of a producer than a reporter. I try to stay behind scenes whenever possible. Now, as far a name goes…" The man paused for a moment, then smiled as if he was letting him in on a secret, like he had a few names to choose from. "For now, you can think of me as Gordon J. Miller."

"And what exactly do you do in your real job, Mr. Miller, when you're not flying around in helicopters and looking at these damn crazy crop circles? From the way you chased off those junior G-men, I can guess you got some experience dealing with strange cases."

"You pegged it right, guy," he said. "I'm an investigator."

"What kind of investigator?"

"A dead serious one."

"That I can see," Freeman said. "I'm glad you're here."

When the reporter headed back toward the field, Freeman crossed the road and went up to the farmhouse. He could use another break from watching the crop-circle watchers.

He could also use some straight answers from the sheriff. He remembered what Sanger said about being tied up with reporters and he didn't want to make a pest of himself so soon after the last call. So instead of calling him up right away, he counted down for a full minute before he got him on the phone once again.

"What is it now, J.D.?" the sheriff said. His voice sounded a bit less harried than last time. Maybe he'd chased the reporters off.

"It's about this fella out here, name of Gordon J. Miller. Cut from a different cloth than the others. He said I should give you a call and talk things over."

"Figured that might happen," Sanger said. "What do you want to know?"

"Well, to start with," Freeman said, "I'm guessing he's some kind of military. Not a desktop soldier, but the real thing."

"Trust this guy and anyone he vouches for."

"He said practically the same thing about you, Sheriff."

"See? The man knows what he's talking about. Shoot straight with him and he'll shoot straight with you."

"I'll do that, Sheriff."

SHORTLY PAST NIGHTFALL Mack Bolan rapped at the rear door of the farmhouse and waited ten seconds before Freeman opened it just enough for him to slip inside.

The farmer glanced down at the satchel Bolan was carrying. "Hello, Gordon. Planning on staying awhile?"

"Until this thing's over."

"Then come on into the kitchen and set yourself down," Freeman said. "I've got some coffee on."

Bolan followed him into a long narrow kitchen that looked out the back of the farmhouse. There was a large iron stove that took up the center of the room, and off to the side was a sturdy wooden table with two ceramic mugs and a bottle of whiskey.

Freeman grabbed the metal coffeepot from the stove and poured the cups two-thirds of the way to the top. "How strong you take your coffee?" the farmer asked as he poured two fingers of Irish whiskey into his own cup.

"This'll do fine for now," Bolan said, sliding his cup across the table before Freeman could add a bit of Irish to it. He nodded his head at the whiskey bottle and said, "I'll take you up on that another time."

"Fair enough," Freeman said. He sipped his coffee, then sat back into his chair. "Now let's have that talk. The Sheriff paid me a visit before and helped explain what was going on, as far as he knows anyway. But I imagine you can help fill in the blanks."

"And then some," Bolan said. He cupped his hands around the coffee mug and rolled it back and forth as if he were shaking a pair of dice, taking a gamble on a civilian. Sure the guy was military at one time. But that was a lifetime ago. "First thing, I take it the house is empty."

"I sent the wife to stay with her sister until this thing's over."

"Good," Bolan said. "Now, what about yourself?"

"I'm staying put," Freeman said. "No one's driving me off my land."

"It's your choice," Bolan said. "And if I were in your

place, I'd probably do the same thing. In fact, it'll probably help us if you stay around here and carry on your business as normal.''

''As normal as I can with you guys setting up a shooting gallery out here.''

The soldier nodded. ''There's no other way,'' Bolan said. ''And now that you mention the shooting gallery, I understand you've got at least one gun on the premises.''

''Hell, yes,'' Freeman said. ''Several in fact.'' He nodded toward the other room. ''Got a gun cabinet right in there. Two semiautomatics and a 12-gauge shotgun. And if we really get desperate, there's an old deer rifle that's been in the family for years. Everything's unloaded and locked up tight. Ammunition's locked up in another location.''

''Wise precautions,'' Bolan said. ''Any other time, that is. Right now it might be a good idea to keep both the weapons and the ammunition handy.''

''To shoot aliens?''

''Aliens, angels, storm troops and whatever else is coming your way. Shoot anything out of the ordinary on your property—except for our people.''

''You wouldn't be trying to scare an old man now, would you?''

''That's part of it, yeah, just to make sure you know what's at risk here. You see, Mr. Freeman—''

''Call me J.D.,'' Freeman said.

''Done,'' Bolan said. ''You see, J.D., when they come back, they'll be totally concentrating on you this time, not on the field they were carving their initials in.''

''You mean *if* they come back.''

''No,'' Bolan said. ''They're already here.''

Freeman looked startled. He glanced at the field out back. ''You mean out there?''

''Not there and not yet,'' the soldier said. ''But they're looking around. Our surveillance teams had every acre of your property covered since we got word of your encounter with the crop-circle crew. They stay away from your farm during the daylight. They didn't want to take any chances of being spotted. But now it looks like they sent a few MIB teams into the area."

"MIB?"

"Stands for Men In Black."

"Like that movie that came out a while back."

Bolan shook his head. "Nothing like the movie. The Men In Black phenomenon has been around for the last forty years, or maybe even the past two thousand years, if you believe some of the researchers. Despite Hollywood's take on it, in reality the Men In Black are a sinister group of silencers who intimidate and harass UFO witnesses. They usually travel in groups of three and they frequently pose as Air Force officers, intelligence agents or in some cases robotic-like aliens."

"What on earth for?"

"Could be several things," Bolan said. "They might be doing it for disinformation purposes. Or to neutralize hostile witnesses. In some cases they contaminated witnesses with chemical or biological agents that permanently disrupted their nervous system. They've also been known to carry black boxes that somehow interfere with the victim's brain waves. By the time they leave, the witness can no longer recall the real details of their experience."

The farmer sighed and sat back in his chair. He subconsciously moved his chair farther away from the window, as if he could see the MIB heading for him. "If you guys know so much about this group, why haven't you been able to stop them?" Freeman asked.

"That's why I'm here," the Executioner said. He reached down to the satchel at his feet and tugged open the side pocket. Then he took out an eight-page newsletter printed on heavy card stock and slid it across the table. "Here," he said. "Take a look at this. It says it a lot better than I could. Maybe it'll help you decide the best course to follow."

The newsletter was a monthly publication put out by Nicodemus Vril. Freeman flipped through the newsletter, stopping when he saw the photograph of the radio host on one of the inside pages. "I know this guy. Seen him on television now and then. Heard him on the radio late at night when I'm flipping the channel. He's a nut, isn't he?"

Bolan shrugged. "Some people think so. I've found him to be one of the most straightforward men I've ever met. A down-to-earth guy in an out-of-this-world field. He holds no illusions about what's out there."

"You mean he's not a true believer?"

"He knows something strange is going on," the Executioner said. "He's just not sure what it is. He doesn't want to label it—he just wants to find it."

Freeman leafed through the newsletter again and stopped when he came to the centerfold article. The byline was by Nicodemus Vril.

Bolan leaned across the table and watched him read the article that he almost knew by heart.

Back in Black

The Unearthly Evolution of the Men In Black

by

Nicodemus Vril

In the uncertain world of UFO research there is only one thing you can be certain of. If you are lucky—or unlucky—enough to be a witness to a genuine UFO, one day you will be visited by three strangely dressed Men In Black, or MIB, as they are commonly referred to by insiders.

This unsettling visit may occur before you've even reported the sighting to authorities. There have been cases where witnesses to a sighting have found the silencers waiting for them at their door before they've even returned home from the sighting. However, according to the majority of the reports, the first visit usually occurs shortly after you make an official report to the Air Force, police department or even the local news station.

The MIB, or Silencers, as they are also known, have been around for at least fifty years, ever since the UFO flap over the state of Washington when several shining discs were seen...

While Freeman turned the page and kept on reading, Bolan glanced through the dark window at the fields beyond. The only dangerous force out there right now belonged to him. A number of COG operatives had taken up position along the banks of the stream and any other shelters they could find. They were wearing their infrared-resistant suits to keep from being spotted by any UFORCE craft flying overhead.

When he was finished reading the newsletter article, Freeman pushed it away from him as if it were a letter bomb.

"Christ, Gordon. Why didn't anyone tell me about this before?"

"We're telling you now," Bolan said. "There's still time for you to get out of this thing if you act right away. We can have someone double for you, and no one will know the difference."

Freeman looked hard at Bolan and took in his confident and poised manner in the face of a lethal firestorm. "You've done this before, haven't you?" he asked.

"Yeah, I have," Bolan said. "A few times."

"Then I guess I'll stick with you."

The Executioner nodded. "That's exactly what we figured would happen. But I wanted you to know what you're facing here so you could make an informed choice. Granted, you had a lot of military experience, but that was a long time ago. You got used to civilian life and there's no need for you to give it up."

"I'm not the running kind."

"What's coming is a strike team. The MIB recon units have thoroughly canvassed the area by now and reported back to their superiors. So far the story hasn't got out about the Gray you unmasked. They'll want to keep it that way."

"They'll be coming to silence me," Freeman said. He tapped the newsletter on the table. "Just like Vril's article said."

"There's a couple of scenarios they might try," Bolan said. "If they want to make you disappear forever, they'll just come in and snatch you in the middle of the night. Then they'll spread some rumors about a ship taking you away to join the cosmic brotherhood. Before you know it, the disappearance of J. D. Freeman will be just as famous as the crop circle on his farm."

"I'm not the traveling kind," Freeman said. "What's the other scenario?"

"Full-scale abduction," Bolan said. "They'll take you away just long enough to change your mind about what you saw the other night. According to the intel we've gathered, they'll try drugs, implants, psychic driving or a combination of all three. When you're all tuned up, they'll send you back here to spread whatever disinformation they programmed into your brain."

"But why do it?" Freeman said. "Why risk coming back for me?"

"Who's going to stop them?"

He looked hard at Bolan. "You are. I hope."

"Yeah," Bolan said. "But they don't know that yet. Let's get ready for when they come. I'll explain what's going to happen."

"What's the plan?"

"We're going to catch a UFO," the Executioner said as if it were the most logical thing in the world.

THE BLACK HELICOPTERS knifed across the Colorado sky.

Like droning metal hornets zeroing in on their target, they flew in straight lines just above the contours of the earth. Rotor wash from a half-dozen helicopters bent the treetops as the UFORCE squadron skimmed across the forests.

Every time they crested a ridge, the choppers dropped low and swooped down across the open farmland.

They were all flying black. No lights to give away their

presence. Engine-suppressor systems to reduce visibility to in-frared sensors.

The black squadron soared through the night, moving ever closer to Freeman's farm, thoroughly convinced it was cloaked from detection.

INSIDE THE FARMHOUSE Freeman sat in his living room watching the airborne armada on his television set.

"I don't believe it," he said, looking at what was coming across the screen. The COG specialists from the technical services division had rigged the twenty-seven-inch television to display a combined video feed from their surveillance monitors.

"Believe it," Bolan said. "They're coming."

The black helicopters had been detected in an invisible cross fire of satellite beams and ground sensors that enveloped Freeman's farm and the entire region around Ballard Mills. The faint signatures of the helicopters showed up on the television screen like ghostly images from a video game.

Although UFORCE normally was hard to spot due to its advanced stealth crafts, this time around Hal Brognola's ELINT task force had advance warning and knew where to look. With technical assistance from the NORAD base at Cheyenne Mountain in northern Colorado, the big Fed was able to saturate the targeted airspace with a low-signature surveillance umbrella that picked up the helicopters in the Mesa Verde region and plotted their route to Freeman's farm.

The Executioner studied the television screen and saw that the chopper squadron was drawing near. "We've got about five minutes before they get here," Bolan said. "Let's get into position."

"What about the television set?"

"Keep it on. We'll let them think that you feel asleep in front of the tube. Easy pickings for aliens."

Freeman nodded, then picked up the 12-gauge shotgun he'd taken from the gun cabinet earlier. He followed the soldier to the back of the house. "You sure they won't be able to see us in these things?'' Freeman asked, looking down at the climate-controlled suit he had been given to wear. It was lightweight despite all of the gadgetry built into it.

''Not until it's too late,'' Bolan said.

THE UFORCE CHOPPERS SLOWED as they crossed the final field. Below them the crop circle shone in the moonlight like the target of a bull's eye.

The two choppers on the extreme left and right flanks spread out and dropped down practically on top of the crop circle. UFORCE soldiers with submachine guns and flak jackets jumped down from the helicopters and spread out across the field. As soon as the men disembarked, the helicopters went aloft again, hovering silently near the crop-circle zone.

The four other gunships proceeded straight across the road, lowering drop lines as they neared the house.

Gray shapes slid down the lines like spiders and dropped softly to the grass. The ''aliens'' ran to the farmhouse, reaching it before the other helicopters set down on the grass.

THE EXECUTIONER WATCHED the Grays circle the house and climb up on the porch. Some of them drifted close to the windows on the side of the house where the television set was still flickering. As they peered inside, their long fingers splayed out upon the glass.

If he hadn't been prepared for it, Mack Bolan could have very easily believed he was witnessing an alien invasion.

The soldier was lying almost prone on the edge of the riverbank, tracking the stainless-steel barrel of the Accuracy International PM sniper rifle across the killzone. The box magazine had twelve 7.62 mm rounds. He could take out some of the Grays if necessary, but his main targets were the pilots of the black choppers.

One of the gunships was on the ground less than sixty yards away from him. After dropping its cargo of Grays, it had landed with its black angular nose toward the house. A faint green glow from the cockpit bathed the faces of the pilot and copilot as they watched the aliens tightening the noose around the house, preparing for the abduction of J. D. Freeman.

The farmer was crouched by the bank about ten yards to Bolan's left, watching the alien assault in amazement, clutching his shotgun and thanking God that he was no longer inside the house.

For a moment it was quiet on the field.

Then the first Gray tried to go through the front door. It exploded outward with a thunderous crash that swept him off the porch and sent him flying for about ten feet before he came down. The entire front of his Gray costume disintegrated from head to toe, and there was nothing left of him but a bloody shell.

As soon as the booby-trapped door went off, the rest of the porch erupted in flame. The boards popped up like loose piano keys, tumbling end over end into the grass where they smoked and sizzled.

Three Grays landed in the burning heap, but they were beyond pain. The shaped charges had erupted from their feet in a volcanic flash that killed them instantly.

Realizing it was a trap, the surviving Gray commandos ran to the choppers and what they imagined was their ticket out of the dead zone.

But before they even made it halfway home, automatic fire erupted from all along the bank. The steady stream of bullets poured across the field, clanked into the helicopters and scythed through the tall grass.

As the Grays went down in a bloody harvest, the Executioner pulled the trigger of the Accuracy International.

The 7.62 mm round cored a hole through the back of the pilot's neck and went on to shatter the cockpit glass. He slumped forward in his seat.

A UFORCE commando who was about to climb into the open cabin saw the pilot drop and then turned to the bank. A burst of automatic fire ripped from the barrel of his submachine gun and strafed the tall grass near Bolan.

The Executioner buried his face in the dirt. The man was good, he thought. He'd figured out Bolan's position from the entry wound that took out the pilot.

Bolan worked the bolt of the Accuracy International as he moved several yards to his right, keeping his eye on the muzzle-flashes of the commando's submachine gun. He dropped to the ground, raised the long barrel and then took him out with a head shot. The bullet sheared off the upper half of his skull and sprayed his last thoughts into the air. The gunner fell back against the open cabin and lay there with his feet sticking out, suspended a few feet above the cold earth that soon would be his home.

A blizzard of lead plunked into the stream behind Bolan. He turned to his right and saw a half-dozen UFORCE commandos charging down the stream, firing full-auto bursts in a wild zig-zag pattern. They weren't aiming their weapons, but were just spraying the air and hoping for the best.

"Watch out!" shouted the COG trooper to the Executioner's right, and then the words died on his mouth. He was thrown into the water by a burst of automatic fire that laid him out in a backward swan dive.

Two more COG troopers on the other side of the stream were hit by the UFORCE fire and fell back into the tall grass.

Bolan could have used some automatic fire, but the Beretta was slung over his shoulder and if he went for it he'd be dead before he got off a round. He stayed with the Accuracy International, kneeling down on the bank while he worked the bolt. Then he fired from his hip at the closest UFORCE gunman. The 7.62 mm round hammered into the man's chest, spun him around and dropped him face first into the water.

By now the rest of the COG soldiers realized where the counterattack was coming from and they poured fire into the advancing gunmen. The withering volleys shredded the renegade UFORCE soldiers and scattered their bodies across the water.

Seconds later a huge explosion rocked the ground and sent a ball of flame spiraling into the air high above the crop circle.

Bolan looked up and saw an A-10 attack plane screaming over-head to make another assault over the circle.

The A-10 attack planes had been lying in wait, ready to take out anything that landed on the other side of the road. Bolan figured at least one of UFORCE's black choppers had already been knocked out of action. There'd been six to begin with, and only four of them had landed near the house.

That left one more helicopter unaccounted for. But not for long. Another of his A-10 attack planes swooped down in the vicinity of the crop circle. Bright yellow bursts of flame streaked toward the ground from the plane's 30 mm GAU-8 cannon. Another huge explosion rocked the ground, and Bolan saw a fiery pinwheel of molten metal shooting into the sky. The rounds that were fired from the aircraft had a core of depleted uranium that bored through the black helicopter. The heavy fusillade ignited the chopper's fuel tank and flash fried anything that was near it.

Both planes swooped down for one more attack, strafing the ground with rocket fire to knock out any UFORCE troops still on the other side of the road.

The Executioner turned his attention back to the farmhouse. The troopers were swarming across the field, surrounding the helicopters and rounding up any of the survivors. Bolan stepped forward into the high grass, carrying the sniper rifle in one hand and the Beretta in the other. He headed for the chop-per where the pilot he'd shot had slumped forward.

The rotors were still spinning, gradually increasing in speed. There was movement on the other side of the cockpit. The copilot was getting ready to break for it.

As he neared the black helicopter, a face suddenly appeared in the open cabin. In front of it was a long-barreled revolver. Bolan dropped to the ground and fired just as a big chunk of earth exploded beside him.

He rolled and fired up again at the UFORCE commando—just as a deafening roar reverberated behind him. The com-mando was knocked clear out of the other side of the cabin and landed on the ground in pieces.

Freeman stood behind him with his smoking 12-gauge shotgun, amazed at what he'd done.

Bolan was aiming his Beretta at the cockpit when he heard a burst of automatic fire from the opposite side of the copter. COG troopers had seen the threat and reacted. The engine died the same time as the helicopter's copilot.

The Executioner got to his feet and scanned the war zone. Smoke and cordite fumes drifted across the field. The road outside was filling with Army vehicles. Nightfox helicopters were landing outside along the road, dropping off the intelligence units that would interrogate the survivors.

The battle for Freeman's farm was over. Bolan turned toward Freeman. "Thanks for stepping up," he said, remembering how the farmer had stood there behind him and risked everything to help him out.

Freeman nodded. "I couldn't let you do it all yourself," he said. "It's my home. What's left of it." The farmer stared numbly at the front of the house. The fire was out but the porch and the front room were gone. "What do we do now?"

Bolan looked at the back of the house. The kitchen was still intact. In the next few minutes he knew it would become a command post for the covert army descending on the area to figure out the next move. He'd be right in the thick of it.

"I don't know about you," Bolan said. "But right now I could use a cup of that Irish coffee. Hold the coffee."

12

White House War Room, Washington, D.C.

As head of the Justice Department's Sensitive Operations
Group and a number of intra-agency task forces, Hal Brognola
had been in the Commander in Chief's presence on just about
every possible kind of occasion.

Commendations. Complaints. Brainstorming sessions.

This day was one of the more unpleasant occasions.

In the conference room directly below the executive office
suite, Brognola sat in a chair directly across the table from the
President of the United States and waited for his turn to have
his head handed to him.

He sipped the glass of ice water and politely watched the
President work his way up and down the line of military officers and intelligence chiefs gathered in the room.

Right now he was listening to the CIA's station chief from
Mexico City explain that he'd been doing his best to reassure
the Mexican ambassador that the attack on Bastian Dominguez
had nothing to do with the United States. According to the
station chief a lot of influential figures had been out at the
Dominguez estate during the visitation and complained to their
patrons in the Mexican government. Although rumors were
flying about an extraterrestrial encounter in the desert, some of
them believed it was a covert attack orchestrated by U.S.
forces. After all, the leader of the Sonora syndicate and his
drug army had vanished, and Dominguez had long been a target of the current administration.

The President nodded his head throughout the presentation and appeared to be listening calmly. "Tell me something," the President said. "Did they believe you when you told them we had nothing to do with it?"

The chief of station looked surprised at the question. "No," he said. "Of course not. It's just part of damage control."

"I see," the President said. His face reddened quickly, a sign to the initiates that his legendary temper was about to be launched. "Damage control," he repeated. He looked around the table from face to face, checking for reactions.

Before anyone could respond, his hand slashed down onto the table and smacked the hard wood surface with the flat of his palm. Using the hand to push himself up from the chair, he gripped the edge of the table with both hands and leaned dangerously forward. He looked as if he were about to launch himself across the table at the station chief.

"Forget the goddamn damage control!" bellowed the President. "And start inflicting some damage! You can reassure the ambassador and the prime minister and anyone else you talk to that Bastian Dominguez is the first of many to come, unless they help us find the UFORCE base down there. I can't believe this. You're actually apologizing to the Mexican government because someone took out the leader of one of the most murderous cartels in the hemisphere? Too bad it wasn't us. Too bad it had to be a UFORCE ship."

The President sat back down and smoothed his hands across the table. The redness began to leave his face. The flare-up was over. As if he hadn't just exploded, the President calmly nodded at the station chief and said in a conversational, friendly tone, "What I'd really like you to do, Jack, is to use some of your charm on our friends below the border. Give them whatever you have to, and see if you can get them to sign on to a joint operation to find this damn ship."

The President turned to Brognola. "Which brings us to you, Hal. I thought we were supposed to end up with the ship in our hands. Instead we blew up half of Freeman's farm. And for what? A half-dozen sneak-and-peek whirlybirds?"

Brognola had been in the hot seat enough times to know that it would do him absolutely no good to argue with the Man. Not yet anyway. His chance would come only after the President went a few rounds with him.

Brognola took the heat, weathering a few rebukes about the Hollywood horror show he'd created down at Freeman's farm and how some of the crash-retrieval units had been shown on national television. To make matters worse, the conspiracy culture was once again talking about black helicopters over America and how the President of the United States was either behind it, or worse, could do nothing about it.

"Actually, Mr. President," Brognola said, when the Man finished taking his shots. "There is something we can do." He mentioned the latest intelligence they received from the captured stealth chopper crews. Some of them had been involved in the cross-border operation down in Sonora. This particular black ops unit always rendezvoused with Goddard's "mother ship" out in open territory. But even though they didn't know exactly where the Mexican base was located, they believed it was somewhere across the border from Sonora in the neighboring state of Chihuahua.

Brognola also explained that some of their more trustworthy contacts in the Mexican intelligence services reported that an insider from the Mexican base had approached them through intermediaries. The alleged insider was worried that he might suffer the same fate as Dominguez and was seeing if he could find a way to avoid it. "It could be smoke and mirrors," Brognola said. "Or it could be the real thing." He nodded down the table at the chief of station. "I'll get together with Jack later to pass on all of our information and see what we can work out together."

"So what you're telling me is you still don't know where Goddard's main ship is," the President said. "Or where his bases are. But you propose to put together a hunting party to traipse across the desert and look under every rock until you find it. Never mind that Chihuahua is the largest state in all of Mexico."

"True, Mr. President," Brognola said. "But we're putting a plan in motion that will lure it out from the Mexican base, if indeed that's where it's currently hiding. We should then be able to identify its location as soon as the ship takes off."

"And how will you perform that miracle?" the President asked.

"Actually, sir," Brognola said. "It won't be me." He looked down the table to his left and said, "Commander Macauley has come up with a plan that will do that for us. It involves the HAARP installation."

Macauley gave Brognola a look that said "Thanks a lot." Then the commander of the Continuity of Government task force turned back to the President, who was now zeroing in on him.

"Is that correct, Commander?"

"Yes, sir," Macauley said. "That is, if we can tap into the HAARP facility based in Alaska—"

"I know where it's based, Commander Macauley. What I don't know is how it can help you find Colonel Goddard and his space cowboys." The President looked around the table and noticed blank looks on some of the faces. "For those of you who don't know, HAARP stands for the High-Frequency Active Auroral Research Program, which has its main site located in Alaska. And if I'm not mistaken, the purpose of HAARP is to enhance military communication systems so we have instant contact anywhere around the globe."

"Yes, sir," Macauley said. "That's one of the stated goals. The other potentialities are still in an experimental phase—"

The President raised his hand. "You're starting to sound like an engineer, Macauley. Just give it to us in plain English."

Macauley smiled. "Of course," he said. "Since its inception, one of HAARP's goals was to use extreme-low-frequency waves to create a virtual mirror in the ionosphere. If we knew the right corridor to search for, the HAARP transmitters could bounce ELF waves off the virtual mirror and down into the corridor below. The signals would then reflect the shapes of stealth craft, no matter how advanced they are, and relay data to satellites, AWACs and ground-monitoring sites.''

The President nodded. ''Why haven't we done this already?''

''Two reasons,'' Macauley said. ''First, this kind of capability is still in the experimental stage, which means it's off limits to most of us. And there are some valid questions about possible harmful effects to the ionosphere by bombarding it with this kind of energy. Second, we haven't had the right corridor to shine the mirror on. It's a great system, but so far it can't cover the entire world at once.''

Brognola listened to the off-the-cuff briefing from the COG commander for the second time today. Earlier when the commander had suggested the possibility of using the system, Brognola saw it as another weapon in the arsenal. As the big Fed watched the growing interest on the President's face, he saw that the Commander in Chief regarded it in the same favorable light.

To avoid confusing the issue, Macauley left out a lot of the more futuristic goals of the HAARP installation. But he did mention its proved ability to alter weather patterns, destroy ballistic-missile guidance systems and inadvertently scramble aircraft navigation systems.

When Macauley finished his briefing, the President clasped his hands in front of him. Then he rested his chin on his steepled fingers while he considered the likely risks and rewards of using the sophisticated but perhaps unreliable system.

Finally the President nodded his head and said, ''We have got no choice. We have got to do whatever it takes to rein in Colonel Goddard. HAARP is no longer off-limits.''

Chihuahua, Mexico

ADOLFO FUERTE STOOD in the hacienda shadows and watched the plumes of dust erupting behind the sand-colored Humvee as it raced across his property. The desert vehicle bounced over the sunbaked earth, carrying yet another group of soldiers to the craggy hills that covered the southern boundary of his Chihuahua cattle range.

Soldiers, he thought darkly. Not Mexican soldiers. Not American soldiers. Enemy soldiers. They were renegades, every one of them, and they had taken part in the great deception.

The Humvee headed straight for the pass through the mile-long plateau that UFORCE had chosen as its base. Land that he was forbidden to trespass upon. In the early days, when he thought the base was empty, he'd sent two of his men to explore the mountain.

The men had never returned. But that night Stevenson showed up on his doorstep and mentioned the need for security at the base. In a deadly serious manner the captain explained that he and the "other ones," as he called the Grays, were counting on Adolfo Fuerte to keep his people away from the site. Stevenson never mentioned what happened to either of the men. And Fuerte had been afraid to ask.

He should have known back then what was coming.

But Fuerte had truly believed there were higher powers on earth. Ever since he was a young man he believed in the powers of magic and sacrifice and witchcraft. After all, had not such things helped him achieve high position in the government? From those beliefs it was only a small leap of faith to accept the existence of an alien presence on the planet. Especially after he'd seen Colonel Goddard's otherworldy ship and the strange weapons that were employed by UFORCE soldiers. At the time he thought such wondrous devices could only be derived from alien technology.

How could he have been so foolish? he wondered.

Fuerte stepped out into the sun to watch the vehicle as it dwindled out of sight. And he wished that he had never seen any of the UFORCE personnel. Especially Goddard.

For too many years he believed in Goddard's fable about the great race of beings that came to earth. Supposedly the aliens were quietly recruiting elite castes from each country to help them create a world government. Fuerte fit that mold. Even though he was no longer an official member of the establishment, he still had contacts at all levels. And he still had the money to reach them.

His years in the government had enriched him beyond his dreams, enabling him to become one of the biggest landowners in central Chihuahua. It was while he was in the government that he encountered the colonel and entered the first of many business deals with him. Most of the deals involved weapons or cocaine, and all of them had been profitable.

But perhaps the most profitable of all was the deal that permitted UFORCE to use part of his property as a base. It fit all of their requirements, and what was more, they told him, they wanted to have someone of his caliber on their side. One day he would be rewarded for his efforts on behalf of the extraterrestrials.

Rewarded with a bullet, he thought. A bullet or whatever they used on Bastian Dominguez. The drug baron had also been a frequent business partner of Goddard, and look what happened to him. Wiped off the face of the earth.

Shortly after Fuerte had agreed to the deal with Goddard, fleets of earthmovers descended on his property. Everywhere he turned, he saw some kind of construction equipment digging up the land. The army of work crews improved the range and graded the roads that led out to Fuerte's main house, using that as a cover for their activities in the hills.

Now he knew more about their other activities, thanks to reports from some of his longtime friends who were at the Sonora encounter.

Aliens, he thought. Not likely. They were just Americans who for some reason had declared war on the upper castes of Mexico. Men like Adolfo Fuerte.

Harsh rays of the sun beat down on his weathered face as he surveyed the land that used to be his. Land that now was Colonel Goddard's.

Perhaps it was time to give them both up, he thought.

Through some of his most trusted contacts, he had passed

word to key officers in the ministry about the possible existence of a secret desert base involved in the Sonora matter. It was an anonymous approach, but from experience, he knew that such secrets couldn't last for long.

Sooner or later he would be found out. But which side would uncover him first?

Santa Fe, New Mexico

THE HOTEL on West Sandoval Street had three hundred rooms, and just about every one was occupied. The annual UFORIA convention had attracted people from all across the country to see the stars of the UFO universe.

Celebrity abductees rubbed shoulders with therapists, hypnotists, skeptics, UFO researchers and past and present government agents. A fair amount of filmmakers and talk-show hosts were also in attendance, either looking for stories or trying to sell their own. And judging from their somber suits and dark glasses, there were even a few MIB in the audience.

Lectures and press conferences were scheduled throughout the day and into the night, presenting a full menu of alien encounters, secret government projects and grainy photos of UFO sightings. If people ever tired of the programs, they could always check out the dealers' room that was sandwiched between two of the larger halls. Books, newsletters, magazines, videotapes, posters, T-shirts and every known bit of alien-oriented paraphernalia were for sale in the packed room.

By three o'clock in the afternoon, Mack Bolan was ready to take the first ship out. But he had business to take care of and a presence to maintain. So he continued to drift in and out of the convention suites and mingle with his fellow researchers. He was wearing an official press badge that bore the name of Gordon J. Miller. And he made sure that every now and then he was seen speaking with Nicodemus Vril as if they were old friends. The host of ''TranceFormations'' played along every time, introducing Bolan to other UFO researchers whenever he got the chance. Vril kept on talking with him until the inevitable happened and he was swept away by some of his fans who were eager to find out the subject of his lecture later in the day.

Bolan's partner in deception, Melissa Rogers, was also making the rounds, seeding her conversations with rumors about the Schyler notebooks and the San Antonio videotapes that were allegedly for sale to the UFO community. She made it clear that she was in the market for them and was willing to pay top dollar.

Rogers handed out business cards to just about everyone she spoke with, making sure they knew that her company was located just across the border in Colorado. She also let it be known that if the sellers wouldn't come to her, she'd go to them, promising that she would personally fly the GFP helicopter anywhere in the continental United States.

Her background in the well-established production company gave her instant credibility. Before long she was becoming something of a celebrity herself. People followed her down the halls and cornered her in the hospitality suite. Whether she wanted it or not, she was going to be the center of attention, sought out by people who either knew someone who had the tapes or else wanted to get the tapes for themselves.

Rogers did a good job of spreading the information around, Bolan thought. It seemed that everyone he talked to already had some idea of what was supposedly on the tapes and in the notebooks. A good number of them claimed that the tapes had visual proof of government involvement in the murder of Dr. Schyler. And they had it on good faith that the notebooks contained handwritten confessions about secret bases and staged alien abductions the psychiatrist had been involved in.

Many of the conventioneers even knew the name of the shadowy group that was allegedly behind the killings. The Executioner frequently heard UFORCE whispered as he passed by small groups.

It was working better than he expected. All of the press about UFORCE was bound to prod them into action. He was fairly certain they'd take the bait. And he'd be ready for them when they made their move.

By four o'clock in the afternoon the soldier was ready for a break.

Bolan went into the hospitality room and grabbed a cup of strong black coffee. Then he wandered into one of the larger convention rooms that literally had the best seats in the house. He dropped into a cushioned chair in the back of the room and drank his coffee while he scanned the crowd.

At first the Executioner was more interested in the audience than he was in the speaker, but he eventually found himself paying attention to the gray bearded sociologist up on the podium.

With his faded leather vest and denim shirt rolled halfway up his thick forearms, the speaker looked more like a biker than an academic. His long but sparse white hair probably hadn't been cut since the sixties and gave him the air of a wild-eyed revolutionary.

"The military is in league with aliens," the speaker was saying. He spoke with such conviction that nearly half of the people in the audience were nodding their heads along with him. "We've got firsthand evidence of their collaboration. In fact, I was recently shown a tape of an underground installation…"

It sounded to Bolan as if the man were describing the UFORCE base that he and the COG troopers had overrun. But as the man spun out his story, it became clear that he was either making it up from whole cloth or just adding a few details to the hoary old stories that had been making the rounds for the past forty years.

About ten minutes into the man's presentation he brought one of his collaborators on stage. Bolan had seen her walking around before and had also seen her photograph in the program brochure. She was one of the star abductees. She wore a dark brown sweater that clung to her statuesque figure and a light tan skirt with dark stockings. The sociologist began asking her questions about her abduction by aliens, which he supposedly uncovered during a hypnotic regression session.

It was obviously a stand-up routine the two had worked out ahead of time, designed to paint her encounter as an amorous adventure rather than the painful experiences most of the "real" abductees spoke about.

While it was an entertaining bit of theater, it certainly had nothing to add to the UFO knowledge base, Bolan thought. But it sure would add to her bankroll. As the starlet repeated several times at the end of her presentation, her book about her rapturous encounters was available in the dealer's room. She would also be available, she purred into the microphone, to sign copies, grant media interviews and pose for pictures. What a surprise, Bolan thought.

He glanced down at his watch.

It was almost five o'clock.

Show time was just a half-hour away. That was when Nicodemus Vril had agreed to meet with him and the two guests that Hal Brognola brought to the convention under armed guard.

The rooms assigned for the meeting were on the top floor of the hotel in a VIP wing that had been paid for by Ground Force Productions. The only access was by a private elevator.

Bolan stepped inside the elevator car and nodded at the operator, who was one of Brognola's plainclothes security men. A minute later he was on the top floor, where two more security men stood outside the corner room.

Both of the security operatives had their holstered side arms visible and within easy reach.

The Executioner walked past them and used his magnetic card to open the door. Another security operative stood directly in his path.

Behind him Bolan could see the now famous videographers Janice Regan and Lazarus Erasque sitting at a long U-shaped leather couch that faced an elaborate entertainment center. Neither of them looked up. In the past twenty-four hours they'd spent a lot of time in the presence of Brognola and the Executioner. The security precautions were second nature to them by now.

"It's me," Bolan said to the guard.

"Just checking," the guard responded, stepping out of the way and closing the door.

Regan looked away from the large blue television screen display that was cued to play the tape. "Is he coming?" she asked.

"Soon," Bolan said. "Are you ready?"

The spiky-haired video stringer laughed and grabbed Erasque by the shoulder. "Since the day we were born," she said.

TEN MINUTES LATER Nicodemus Vril stepped into the highly guarded hotel suite. He looked at Bolan, then at the guard who stayed by the window watching him.

"Why all the cloak and dagger?" Vril asked.

Bolan waved at the pair on the couch. "Because of them." As they stood, he said, "I'd like you to meet the people who caught the San Antonio killings on tape. This is Janice Regan and Lazarus Erasque. Self-proclaimed video guerrillas."

Regan took Vril's hand in hers and led him toward the television set. "And this is our tape," she said. She pressed the remote-control unit and the tape began.

Vril sat and watched the night-vision footage of the police slaying outside Dr. Schyler's building. He didn't say a word from beginning to end, staring at the screen like a hypnotized man. When it was over, he said, "Oh, my God. Oh, my God... I've got to have it."

"It's yours," Bolan said.

"What?" Vril said. "But it belongs to them. You said so yourself."

"They've already made a deal with the government," Bolan said. "You're part of it. They trust you to do the right thing."

"Oh, my God," Vril repeated. "This is incredible. You had something to do with this, didn't you?"

"A bit," Bolan said. "Something to keep all sides happy.

They get protection and a substantial reward for turning over the tape to the proper authorities. You get an exclusive when this is all over.''

"I see," Vril said. "And when will that be?"

"Soon, we hope," Bolan said. "As soon as we set this thing in motion."

THE SEVEN-O'CLOCK SESSION was packed. People were standing in the halls outside the convention room, lining up to see Nicodemus Vril. Word had spread that he had a major announcement to make.

He wasted no time. As soon as he stepped onto the stage, he grabbed the mike and said, "Ladies and gentleman, there's been a lot of talk at this convention about a videotape of the San Antonio slaughter that may or may not be circulating. A tape that may or may not be up for sale. Well, let me tell you right off that the tape exists. And let me tell you that it will soon be in my possession."

A chorus of gasps and murmurs spread through the audience.

"Let me tell you that in addition to the tape I'll also have the notebooks you may have heard of," Vril continued. "The Schyler notebooks. It's part of a package deal that is currently being negotiated with a media consortium. Now, I want everyone to understand that I don't yet have either of these items in my possession. As I'm sure most of you can appreciate, these are delicate negotiations."

Vril paused for a moment and looked out over the gathered audience, knowing that every last one of them was in the palm of his hand.

"Two things I can tell you," Vril said. "I have seen the tape. I have seen the notebooks. Held them in my hands, ladies and gentlemen. They are real and they are frightening."

He paused long enough for the audience to feel the chill. "The other thing I can tell you is that it will not belong exclusively to me. This other party, which has very strong media connections, will eventually produce a documentary, or series of documentaries, about the subject. Yours truly will most likely be the narrator for these fascinating bits of film history. Of course I will break the story on my radio show and will be the first in the country to have the inside story of what's really been going on. At last the answer to one of the greatest UFO mysteries of all time will be in our grasp.''

Realizing that he was approaching the border of oratorical excess, he scaled back the excitement in his voice. ''And of course I realize that I can't be alone in this. If there is anything of a sensitive nature, a national-security aspect, for instance, rest assured that I will consult with the proper authorities before going public with the story of the decade.''

Vril clapped his hands together and then looked out at the audience. ''Well, that's the start of my presentation tonight. Before I go any further, are there any questions?''

As the television cameras rolled and flash cameras went off, Vril played to his audience. He forced himself to keep a smile on his face throughout the rest of his presentation, even though now and then he found himself scanning the crowd for some of the faces he knew were out there.

UFORCE was watching.

And he was inviting them to play the most dangerous game of his life.

13

Durango, Colorado

There were no lights on in the studio complex on Camino del Rio when Melissa Rogers swung her BMW into the staff parking lot and drove up to the side door to Ground Force Productions. She switched off the engine, then hurried to the entrance, fishing inside her pocketbook for a jangling key ring. It took her only a second to find the right key and unlock the door.

It was just past ten o'clock at night, and the deserted stairwell echoed loudly as she climbed up the concrete steps to the second floor.

When she entered the upstairs hallway it seemed even more tomblike. Soundproof walls sealed off most of the GFP recording studios and offices from the sounds of the outside world.

Rogers hurried down the hallway to her office, unlocked the door, and then reached for the light switch on the wall.

"Don't turn on the light. It's better this way."

Her hand froze on the wall. The shadowy figure of a man was sitting behind her desk.

"Sit down," he said in the soothing, deep voice she recognized from the call to her cellular phone earlier in the evening. "We've got some things to discuss."

In the moonlight shining through the windowpane she saw a short-haired man in a dark business suit.

"Who are you?" she said in a wavering voice. "What are you doing here?"

"You know who I am," the intruder said. "The name's Chet, remember? It wasn't that long ago we talked. "

"Yes."

"Then you know why I'm here. We've got an appointment."

"Yeah," she said. "But the appointment was for eleven and it's only a few minutes past ten. And when you suggested we meet in my office, I assumed I'd be the one sitting behind my desk waiting for you."

He shrugged. "You shouldn't assume anything about me. Just like you shouldn't assume that your security locks and alarms can keep a guy like me out of here."

"I'm impressed," she said. "Now, what about the tape? Where is it?"

The man stared hard at her, obviously surprised by her response. He gestured at the chair by the desk. "Sit down," he said. "Please. Sorry for doing it this way, but in my line of work you have to take precautions. It's better off for all concerned if no one sees us together."

Shaking her head at how easily she ceded control of the meeting, she sat in the chair facing him and placed her pocketbook on her lap. "Your line of work," she said. "Would that happen to be the government?"

"I'm not at liberty to say."

Rogers nodded her head. "That's what everyone in the government says."

"Yeah, well, it's no secret we're interested in the San Antonio tapes and the notebooks. It's a matter of national security."

"It always is with you guys."

"This time it's real. We have to make sure these sensitive materials don't fall into the wrong hands. But it looks like we've got a misunderstanding here," he said. "I thought you had the tapes."

"I do," she said. "I mean, I don't have them yet, but they're as good as ours. We're still negotiating for them."

"With who?"

"Actually," she said, "I'm still not sure who the sellers are. They're using another party to handle the details. When you called before, I thought maybe you were working with them. Trying to arrange a separate deal."

The man tapped his hand on the desk. "Like maybe a deal that cut Vril out of the action?"

She shrugged. "That's why I'm here. I don't usually make a habit of holding clandestine meetings in my office. But how do you know we're dealing with Vril?"

The man shrugged. "It's a bit obvious. You were seen huddling together at the Santa Fe convention. And then during his speech he came right out and said he was in some kind of partnership with a media company…"

"Almost a partnership," she said. "It's not a done deal yet, mainly because they haven't handed over the tape or the notebooks. And as far as the partnership goes, it's pretty one-sided. We'll end up laying out most of the money, and Vril will take in most of the profits."

"Would you consider selling the materials to us?" the man asked. "That is, if you're capable of getting them?"

"If the price is right."

"Oh, it will be. We can outbid you and Vril put together."

"It's not a matter of outbidding anyone," Rogers said. "The sellers came to Vril because they know and trust him. On the other hand they've never heard of me or my company. And you…you're someone who sneaks into buildings in the middle of the night. Hardly inspires trust, you know?"

"We've got unlimited funds at our disposal. You can write your own ticket. Just try and contact them. See if you can cut Vril out of the picture and bring the goods to us."

"If I get a chance between now and Wednesday I will."

"What happens then?"

"According to Vril, that's when they're delivering the package."

"Where?"

"Where else?" she said. "Reality Base."

"Isn't that what he calls his radio station?"

"Yeah," Rogers said. "He's going to premiere it on his show."

FROM A THIRD-FLOOR WINDOW across the street from the GFP complex, Mack Bolan watched the intruder's face through the Bender scope mounted on the Accuracy International sniper rifle. The barrel rested on the windowsill at just the right downward angle.

Another shooter was zeroed in on the same target from the next window over. They'd been ready for the killshot ever since the man who identified himself as Chet arrived at the studio and thought he was breaking in unnoticed.

There was a backup team covering the side door and the rear exit just in case the meeting went sour.

But judging from the miked conversation Bolan had been listening to on his headset, the man was convinced he found a greedy soul mate in Melissa Rogers. He thought she was willing to sell out Vril and the owners of the tape as long as the money was right.

Through the headset, the Executioner heard them wrapping up their conversation.

"Got a number I can reach you at?" Rogers asked.

The man laughed. "I'll reach you," he said. "Just see if you can come up with something."

The UFORCE man who'd identified himself as Chet walked to the door, unaware that the crosshairs of Bolan's sniper scope followed him every step of the way. They'd all recognized him instantly as one of the three rogue operatives who'd been caught on the San Antonio tape.

As soon as Rogers closed the door behind him, she looked

at the windows where Bolan and the other shooter had been waiting. "Let me know when he's gone for good," she said.

She reached into her pocketbook and took out the automatic that had never been too far from her fingers throughout the entire meeting. Then she sat at her desk and aimed the automatic at the door.

The man who'd tried to pass himself off as a government agent left through the side door, then walked down to the corner. Bolan watched him walk away, knowing that he'd be kept under a loose surveillance for the next couple of days. But even if they lost him, the Executioner suspected he'd see him again out at Reality Base.

Monticello, Utah

"KEEP IT RUNNING," Colonel Goddard shouted to the pilot of the HeloTours chopper when it touched down on the helipad near the small terminal building.

As he headed for the entrance, he looked with satisfaction out at the maintenance yard where a crew of mechanics was overhauling the fleet of company choppers. The tour helicopters not only made a profit for the UFORCE front company, but they also provided cover for the times when he had to move a lot of his people around without attracting too much attention.

Like now.

Located in the southeast corner of Utah, near the Four Corners border with Colorado, New Mexico and Arizona, the tour company was one of several that prospered in the area. No one had given it a second thought.

Stevenson was waiting for him just inside the terminal. He was holding a videotape in his hand.

"Is that what I think it is?" Goddard said, nodding at the tape.

"No," Stevenson replied. "It's not the San Antonio tape. As far as we know that one's still on the market."

"Then why'd you bring it?"

Stevenson waved the tape as if it were a winning ticket in the lottery. "This could be just as important. I thought you'd want to see it right away."

"What is it?"

"It's from the Santa Fe convention."

Goddard gave him a withering look. "I've already been briefed on that."

Stevenson shook his head. "Not on this. Some of our people in the crowd put it together. One of them was posing as a TV reporter, the others as UFO fanatics with cameras. They caught something you should see."

Goddard followed him into a small office that looked out onto the maintenance yard, then watched patiently as the captain loaded the videocassette into a desktop unit.

The screen came to life a moment later, showing the crowds moving in and out of the convention halls and milling about some of the celebrity guests.

Stevenson grabbed the remote control, pressed the fast-forward button and then froze the tape when it came to rest on a rugged-looking man with a press pass clipped to his shirt.

"Who's that?" Goddard asked.

"Name tag says he's a guy called Gordon J. Miller. Supposed to be an investigator. We looked into his background, saw that he's done some articles about UFOs and he seems to know some of the big names in the field."

"Seems to?"

"Right," Stevenson said. "We're not sure he really is what he says he is. We just might have two different guys here." The captain forwarded the tape to a spot that showed the man sitting in the back of one of the convention halls. The camera lens had zoomed in on him, showing a better close-up of his face.

It was a hard and weathered face with bracing eyes that scanned the room like a military man or a cop. "See," the captain said. "Here we've got a hard-looking guy you wouldn't want to mess with. And here—'' He forwarded the tape until it showed the same guy talking with Nicodemus Vril and another one of the conference lecturers ''—we got a guy who's hamming it up with the big shots.''

''So he's talking to Vril and laughing it up,'' Goddard said. ''Everyone does that when Vril's around.''

''Yeah. This guy looks like he's laughing but he's got something on his mind.''

The colonel laughed. ''Are you a mind reader now, Captain? Is this a talent you haven't disclosed before?''

''Just bear with me,'' Stevenson said. ''One of our guys who reviewed the tape thought he looked familiar, as if maybe he'd seen him at the Brognola briefing down at that quarry place. If he's right and the guy was down there, it means he's some kind of military. Covert military.''

Goddard nodded. It wasn't hard to picture the alleged investigator in that role. He didn't look like the kind of guy who went around asking questions for a living. He looked like someone you asked questions about.

''So I went through the tape a couple of times,'' Stevenson continued. ''And then the guy starts to look familiar to me, too. Not the way he looks now. That's different. But the way he moves and acts. I think I've seen this guy before myself.''

''When?''

''Back when I was leg—''

''Legit?'' Goddard asked.

''Right,'' the captain said. ''On the side of the red, white and blue.''

''You're still on that side,'' Goddard said. ''They're the ones who've gone wrong by trying to destroy us, the only force that can truly defend our country. Our—''

''You don't have to convince me, Colonel,'' Stevenson said. ''I'm still here, aren't I?''

''Yes, of course,'' Goddard said. He glanced back at the tape. ''Go on. Where'd you see him before.''

''It was a joint task force,'' Stevenson said. ''A special-ops mission headed by Brognola. This Gordon Miller guy almost looks like one of the soldiers who went with us. Guy went by the name of Belasko back then. According to some of the other guys on our team, he was also known by another name. The Executioner.''

The colonel's eyes widened at the mention of the legendary warrior. He actually looked pleased. "So they sent the Executioner after us," said. "I heard he was dead."

"Or he just went into deep cover," Stevenson said. "Like us. The thing is, I'm not really sure who he is. He spent a lot of time in Vril's company so maybe he is just another investigator. It could also mean he's a front man for the people selling the tapes to Vril. Hell, he might even be a buyer trying to get them for himself. Could be a lot of reasons why a guy like that's been hanging around the circuit.''

"A while ago you thought it was him," Goddard said. "Now you're trying to talk yourself out of it. What's your gut tell you?"

"I think it's him but I can't guarantee it," the captain said. "Guy's probably changed a lot since I saw him. It was a long time ago when we went out on that operation. Since then he could of had some changes done to him. Plastic surgery. War wounds. Who knows?''

Goddard folded his arms behind his back and walked to the window, where his sun-struck reflection looked back at him. Gut instincts were important to men in his business. They often lived or died by them.

The colonel stayed by the window for a long time, quietly thinking over his options. He stood perfectly still in front of the reflection, as if carrying on an internal debate.

"Let's say it is the Executioner," Goddard finally said, turning away from the window. "That makes him one of the most potent weapons they can send against us. What if we turn it against them? What if we get him working for us?''

Stevenson shook his head. "A guy like that won't turn. Not at any price."

"I don't mean voluntarily," the colonel said. "I mean give him the abduction treatments and see how he responds. We can adapt it any way you want."

The captain shrugged. "We can try, but even if we manage to take him alive, he's not going to be an easy subject. The treatments might not hold. Even if we go the implant route, it's still unreliable. A strong-willed guy like that...I think he'll break before he'll ever respond."

"Then we'll just have to break him," Goddard said. "And then we'll break Brognola. After that we'll start naming our terms."

Stevenson turned off the videotape and popped it out of the machine. He rapped the black plastic case with his knuckles. "Whoever this guy is, I have a feeling we're going to find out real soon."

"What do you mean?"

"Some of our people were out in Black Wall, casing the town and Vril's radio station."

"And?"

"The guy on this tape has also been spotted in the town. That means he's either a buyer, a seller or...the Executioner."

"Good," Goddard said. "Whoever he is, he's ours."

Black Wall, New Mexico

MACK BOLAN DROVE the white Range Rover out of town, following the long straight road that led out to Nicodemus Vril's base. He knew the territory well from his previous recons.

Two miles outside of town he thought someone was following him. The sun was glinting off a car windshield about a quarter-mile behind him. He kept his foot on the pedal, going the same speed.

It could be a real driver just getting out of town for a while, Bolan thought. It could also be a tail by one of the UFORCE commandos they'd detected around Black Wall the past couple of days.

But it was Wednesday and that made him suspicious.

This night Nicodemus Vril was scheduled to do his thing. That meant there would soon be a lot stronger UFORCE presence in the area.

Bolan wouldn't be alone in the target zone when they made their move. There already was a unit stationed out at Reality Base. And Brognola had other teams on standby, ready to launch them into action.

Brognola also had the HAARP surveillance umbrella in place. From what Bolan understood about the system, it could cover a large swath of land. Hypothetically the HAARP net would detect any kind of stealth craft the moment it crossed over into that corridor. Hypothetically they'd have plenty of warning when Goddard was in the area.

The problem was, Bolan thought, there were too many hypotheticals floating over his head. From his last briefing with Brognola, Bolan knew the HAARP net already had been cast over the central Chihuahua area. And it had been found lacking. The Mexican authorities had tipped them to the location of the base when one of their cartel cronies, Adolfo Fuerte, finally came clean about the hidden installation on his property. HAARP had been targeted on the zone as soon as word came in.

But the HAARP net came up empty. By the time the joint American and Mexican task force swept into the desert base, the bird had already flown. Either it had left the base before HAARP was tasked to the area, or it was sophisticated enough to escape detection.

And that was the kind of ship Bolan was hoping would show up over Nicodemus Vril's high desert complex. He had a feeling he'd get what he was wishing for...but he didn't know if he'd survive it.

He looked in the mirror and saw that the car was gaining on him.

Bolan was still several miles away from Vril's turnoff. It could be anybody following him. But the Executioner reached down for the holstered Beretta on the seat beside him and flicked the selector to full-burst mode.

If the car came upon him quickly, he wasn't going to have too much reaction time. That meant he wanted to spray as much lead as possible.

He kept his head straight, only glancing in the mirror now and then to check on the progress of the tail car. He didn't want to give away his suspicions until the last possible second.

While Bolan was watching the car, he saw a dark shadow silhouetted against the sky far off to his right.

A helicopter.

The shadow moved closer. It was heading on a path that would intersect with the road just about the same time that the car behind him caught up to the Range Rover.

Bolan eased up on the gas pedal and let the car gain on him. He held the barrel of the weapon on the armrest. It would only take a split second to raise it and fire at the passing car.

The car accelerated suddenly and drove past him. The only menacing thing about the car was the driver, who scowled at him for slowing down. The car sped out of sight.

A moment later the helicopter crossed the road in front of him. It was low enough so he could make the lettering on the side panels.

HeloTours.

Maybe it was a group of UFO fanatics who'd chartered a flight out to Vril's place, hoping to drop in on him for the momentous occasion. Could be, he thought. But he decided to pass the name of the chopper to Brognola as soon as he reached Vril's place and could use the secure comm line.

A SHADOW MOVED across the Utah desert.

It was shaped like a black manta flowing across the desert sands. But there was nothing in the sky to cast the shadow.

At least that was how it appeared to the commando unit that waited for it to land. The bottom of the Borealis was the same color as the sky above it. The digitally camouflaged skin on the underside of the craft projected a constantly shifting palette of sky. The upper body of the angular ship was coated with a desert-colored skin that perfectly matched the ground below.

When the ship landed, the men grabbed their advanced assault weapons from the jeeps that had carried them out to the rendezvous point, then jogged up the ramp into the craft.

Moments later they were part of the shadow that soared across the desert.

Reality Base Radio Network, Black Wall, New Mexico

"AND NOW, ladies and gentleman—and the army of government agents who are listening to the show tonight—it's time to make the announcement you have all been waiting for."

Bolan listened to the voice of Nicodemus Vril from the Green Room just outside of his studio.

"Yes, folks, it is finally in our hands. The most explosive videotape of the century. The one everyone's heard about but no one's seen. It's here at last and we're in the process of transferring it to our Web site. It should be up and running in about an hour or so for those of you who'd like to see for yourselves what we're talking about. Now I must caution you that it is very strong stuff. If you're weak of mind or spirit, it's best not to look at it. It will shock you but it will also educate you to the forces that are trying to run this great country of ours—straight into the ground. We also plan to post the shocking revelations from the notebooks of Dr. Schyler on our Web page so you can read for yourself what's been going on."

Bolan looked through the window at the man sitting behind the microphone.

Sergeant Mowry looked back at him and gave him a thumbs-up. The tall COG trooper was sitting there with his hands on the console and his head near the mike. He was taking over for Vril so it would look like business as usual out at the radio station.

The talk-show host was there in spirit, but not in body. Thanks to the broadcast link set up with GFP studio, Vril was safely running the show from Durango, Colorado. Part of it was scripted by the government, but most of it was pure, uncensored Vril. He knew how to push anyone's buttons, especially the men of UFORCE.

Vril played his part perfectly, the crusader about to expose the sinister plot that held America in its grip. He filled the first hour of the show with a series of long commercial breaks and lengthy recaps about how the tape and the notebooks of Dr. Schyler came into his hands. If necessary, he was prepared to stall for as long as it took before UFORCE showed itself.

But he didn't have to stall at all. The UFORCE invasion began exactly five minutes after the second hour of the broadcast.

THE INVASION BEGAN with an attack from a single helicopter.

The chopper came meandering over the ridge behind Vril's complex. One of the three COG troopers who was watching the rear of the complex called out its arrival to Bolan.

"It's got some kind of markings on the panels," the trooper said, scanning it through his night-vision binoculars. "Hold on, it's getting closer, going to land out back. There, it says HeloTours on the side. It's civilian—"

"Maybe not," Bolan said. He went to the front window, figuring the chopper's arrival might be a distraction for a frontal attack. HeloTours. He didn't like the fact that it hadn't made any approach during daylight hours. He'd called Brognola over the station's secure line and asked the big Fed to look into it. The big Fed's preliminary intelligence indicated that it was a legitimate tour company. But the Executioner wasn't taking any chances.

"Don't let them get too close," Bolan shouted, keeping his eye on the flat stretch of land in front of the station. "Warn them off with a loudspeaker. If that doesn't work, warn them off with a clip.''

"Got it," the man said. "They're getting out. Four of them so far."

From the studio booth, Mowry turned down the audio feed and spoke over the intercom. "Something's happening, Striker. I can feel it. The window's rattling."

The window exploded behind Mowry. The shock wave sent him flying in the air before crashing on the equipment.

Bolan felt another shock wave that sledgehammered into his back and knocked him to his knees.

The other troopers were shouting, dropping to the floor. They, too, had been hit by something.

Bolan staggered to his feet. He was light-headed and had a hard time seeing straight, but he managed to make it to the shattered front window. He gripped the side of the wall by the pane and looked outside.

A dark cloud was drifting toward the station. For a brief moment he saw the outline of a manta-shaped craft. Then it shimmered before his eyes, taking on the hues of the desert and the sky.

The ship was here.

Bolan had a hard time focusing on the ship, on anything at all. He kept his eyes moving and then in the distance he caught a glimpse of the COG backup unit running toward the building. They'd been concealed in a gully just across the road. Good, he thought. He could hold out until they arrived.

But all six men of the backup team suddenly sprawled on the ground, as if they'd been hit by an invisible hand. A shadow passed above them, and the ship returned to the station.

Another shock wave rattled the roof, caving in the beams and smashing the rest of the windows. Bolan jumped back as a large wooden beam slashed the air in front of him like a guillotine.

As he spun around, Bolan caught a glimpse of Mowry. His

hand was still, and it was several inches from his dropped weapon. He looked dead.

Then the Executioner saw four men hurrying for the front of the station. The chopper crew was there.

One of them pointed a long-barreled weapon Bolan's way. The Executioner instinctively lifted his Beretta and squeezed the trigger just as a brilliant light shot through the air.

The first beam passed in front of his face. By the time a second beam shot toward him, he knew what it was. A dazzler. An offensive barrel-mounted laser beam. Pull the trigger and blind the opposition. It worked. Bolan could barely see, although he'd instinctively raised his forearm at the last moment.

He tried to picture the last location of the intruders and where they'd be now, then blindly aimed his Beretta in that direction and yanked back on the trigger, firing again and again until the weapon clicked empty.

Then an acoustic wave ripped into his eardrum. Another pulsed wave smacked into his temple. He felt as if an invisible ray were drilling through his head.

Mack Bolan staggered backward, dropped his weapon and landed on the floor in a heap.

He was down, trying to hold on to consciousness. But it fled just the same. He was out.

CAPTAIN STEVENSON swiftly searched the control room, pushing aside the lanky form sprawled across the console.

No videotapes.

No notebooks.

Not even Nicodemus Vril. The man who'd taken his place was a soldier, not a talk-show host.

It was all a setup.

Stevenson scanned the trashed studio one more time, then looked through the window. There were several UFORCE commandos with advanced assault weapons prowling the zone between the road and the station. The Borealis had dropped them across the road and now they were mopping up the COG troopers. The thick barrels of the UFORCE rifles fired shock waves at hundreds of miles per hour that stunned or killed anything in its path. Along with the dazzlers and the microwave stun guns, they were designed to put the enemy down instantly.

Stevenson watched them work their way back across the road to the rendezvous point.

The Borealis had come in unnoticed, and the HeloTours helicopter had come in plain sight.

He knew that Brognola's crew had a lot more firepower gathered near Black Wall, but they hadn't been able to put it in motion yet. By the time they did, Stevenson and the crew would be gone.

On his way out of the trashed station, the captain looked down at the fallen man in the center of the room. The man was no longer among the living.

"So you're the Executioner," he said to the prone form. "Not anymore, I guess. Not bad, though. We had plans for you."

BOLAN CAME TO just in time to hear the man's taunt. He stayed perfectly still, not breathing, not moving. Just thinking.

When the man walked a few feet away, Bolan tested his body. He recognized that his injuries were caused by prototype shock-wave and acoustic weapons. Stunned muscles. Disorientation. Burns. He had all the symptoms. Obviously the weapons were no longer prototypes. They were part of the regular UFORCE arsenal.

Bolan risked a look at the man who stood just a few feet away from him. It was Stevenson, Colonel Goddard's right-hand man. The man who was caught on the tape giving the signal to execute the San Antonio police officers.

"The vault is empty," Stevenson said into a small radio handset. "We're ready to ride. The bird stays here. Pilot's dead and so's the crew. Pick everyone up on the other side of the road."

As Bolan listened to Stevenson, he moved his hand as quietly as possible to the back of his belt where a thin triple-edged spike was sheathed. His Beretta was too far away, and it was empty.

But there was sufficient strength in his arm to wield the pencil-thin spike. And the man had to walk by him on his way out.

Bolan waited, summoning the strength in his arm, picturing what he had to do.

Stevenson's left foot walked by Bolan's head. He watched the right foot just as it lifted from the floor and then he struck.

He stabbed the spike though the back of Stevenson's foot, right between the tendon and the ankle bone. As soon as the spike came out the other side, Bolan tugged back with everything he had. The big man went down with a splash of blood and a scream of pain.

Stevenson cocked his elbow as he fell to the floor, using his momentum to jam it into Bolan's ribs.

The Executioner felt the cracking of the rib a split second before he felt the river of pain flood through his side.

Bolan was still moving, but so was Stevenson. Both of them were on the floor—and both were going for the kill. Stevenson was swinging his Heckler & Koch submachine gun in an arcing motion that would bring the barrel face-to-face with Bolan.

It was going to be a tie.

But then a shot rang out and Stevenson's body tumbled forward. A spout of blood erupted from his shoulder, and he forgot all about Bolan as he spun at the direction where the shot came from.

Sergeant Mowry had managed to grab his automatic and fire one shot through from the control booth. Stevenson triggered a burst just as Mowry dropped out of sight.

The UFORCE captain swung the barrel back toward Bolan, but the Executioner's hand was already slashing through the air. The end of the spike cored straight through Stevenson's left ear, deep through his brain. Bolan released his grip and watched the man fall to the floor. His head bounced twice and then his dead eyes stared out at a different world. He was dust.

Bolan got to his feet, then made his way to the control booth.

Mowry was lying flat on the floor, dazed from his fall, and surprised to see Bolan standing.

"Come on, guy, get up," Bolan said, reaching his hand out. "Show's over."

AFTER SEEING to the other COG troopers, Bolan raised Brognola on the radio. "What happened, Hal?" he said to the head Fed. "Didn't the ship show up on the HAARP net?"

"Yeah," Brognola said. "We got it as soon as it crossed over into the corridor."

"Why didn't you hit it?"

"Couldn't, Striker. It was right over you."

Bolan remembered the sensation from the first shock waves the ship had fired down at the building and knew how close it had been.

"Well, it's not anymore," Bolan said. "By now it's on its way with the rest of the UFORCE team."

"It's on its way, all right," Brognola said. "It just doesn't know where it's going."

THE CONTROLLERS at the Alaskan HAARP installation tracked the Borealis as it soared back across the Utah skies.

As it crossed the great Salt Lake desert, the controllers bounced an extreme-low-frequency wave from the virtual mirror in the ionosphere. The ELF spike shot down through the Borealis's navigation system, instantly turning it into an explosive mass.

INSIDE THE BOREALIS, Colonel Goddard had only few seconds to realize what had happened. The pilot of the ship was no longer in control. The navigation system was gone. And there was only one direction it could go.

As the nose of the Borealis tilted like a dagger hurtling down to the earth, Goddard could hear the screams of the other men on the craft.

Then he could hear nothing but the roar of the craft as it exploded on impact and sent an aura of flame cascading across the desert, carrying the disintegrating crewmen into infinity.

UFORCE had landed for good.

When all is lost, there's always the future...

JAMES AXLER

DEATH LANDS®

THE SKYDARK CHRONICLES Book III

Shadow Fortress

The Marshall Islands are now the kingdom of the grotesque
Lord Baron Kinnison. Here in this world of slavery and
brutality, the companions have fought a fierce war for survival,
on land and sea—yet the crafty baron still conspires to
destroy these interlopers. They cunningly escape to the neighboring pirate-ruled Forbidden Island, with the baron's sec men
in hot pursuit...and become trapped in a war for total
supremacy of this water world.

Available in September 2001 at your favorite retail outlet.

James Axler

OUTLANDERS®

SARGASSO PLUNDER

An enforcer turned renegade, Kane and his group learn of a mother lode of tech hidden deep within the ocean of the western territories, a place once known as Seattle. The booty is luring tech traders and gangs, but Kane and Grant dare to infiltrate the salvage operation, knowing that getting in is a life-and-death risk....

In the Outlands, the shocking truth is humanity's last hope.

GOUT18

James Axler

OUTLANDERS®

TOMB OF TIME

Now a relic of a lost civilization, the ruins of Chicago hold a cryptic mystery for Kane. In the subterranean annexes of the hidden predark military installations deep beneath the city, a cult of faceless shadow figures wields terror in submission to an unseen, maniacal god. He has lured his old enemies into a battle once again for the final and deadliest confrontation.

In the Outlands,
the shocking truth is humanity's last hope.